The Secret and the Sunday Rose

The Secret and the Sunday Rose

Edited by Katie L. Moran and Jessa R. Sexton
Cover design by Whitnee Webb
Interior design and layout by Whitnee Webb
Illustrations by Anastasia Morozova
Photography by Jessa R. Sexton

Published by:
O'More Publishing
A Division of O'More College of Design
423 South Margin St.
Franklin, TN 37064 U.S.A.

Enjoy the Secret!
Nancy Gentry

The Secret and the Sunday Rose

My sincerest thanks go to Jessa Sexton who, once again, embraced my story, enhanced it with her special talents, and encouraged me. I deeply appreciate how she takes on my projects with a gracious spirit, enthusiastic energy, and high degree of expertise. Many thanks go to Whitnee Webb for her wonderful creativity and the many hours she spent to make my story into a beautiful book of which I am very proud. Thank you also to Anastasia Morozova for using her unique style to create the illustrations which bring my characters to life. And finally, thanks go to Katie Moran for the hours spent in reading my story and fine-tuning it. My wish for all these young women is that they enjoyed using their talents on *The Secret and the Sunday Rose* as much as I did in writing it.

Thank you to all my friends, fellow book-lovers, and storytellers whom I've had the privilege to meet through my story writing for your words of encouragement. I appreciate all the opportunities you have given me through book clubs, book signings, and visits to school groups. You have made my 'author experience' a most memorable one.

No acknowledgement is complete without thanking my family who always support me, share in my joys, and give me a reason to be excited about my books. All the fun comes from being able to share it with my family and friends.

In memory of my dad, Jim Henry Burks

This book is dedicated to my husband and best friend, Earl.

chapter one

The screen door slammed.

Jodie skidded across the kitchen floor on her black patent shoes, which were now more brown than black from the dirt. Mama was standing at the kitchen sink slicing potatoes. Her light brown hair was pulled back at the neck with a yellow ribbon, and her plain yellow dress hung loosely on her thin shoulders. She dropped pieces of potato into the skillet as the grease sizzled loudly and looked up.

Jodie had been so excited and couldn't wait to tell Mama, but now the look on her mother's face stopped her cold. It was that what-am-I-going-to-do-with-you look as her pretty, blue eyes scanned Jodie from head to toe.

Mama gave a tired sigh and said softly, "Jodie, hon', look what you've done to your stockings." She looked down at the potato in her hands. "Again."

Jodie glanced down at the tear and saw her whole knee bulging through the hole in her dark blue stocking.

"I had to slide, Mama," she explained. "But I was safe."

Jodie beamed with pride. Then she blurted out the news.

"And, Mama, I hit a homer!"

Jodie's grin spread from ear to ear. She loved baseball more than anything else in the world. It wasn't her fault that people thought it was a boys' game or that she had to wear stockings and dresses and black patent shoes. She just couldn't resist getting in a game after school. And most of the boys wanted her to play, especially if she was on their team. She could out-hit, out-run, and out-catch most all of them. Only Tommy the Terrible, who was a big bully, and a few of his tag-along friends gave her trouble, and that was only because they didn't like getting beat by a girl.

Mama shook her head and sighed again, but Jodie saw that little twinkle in her mother's eye, the corners of her mouth turning up ever so slightly. Jodie knew she was a mystery to her mother, who was so pretty and thin and fragile. She knew her mother wanted her to be more lady-like, but Mama always seemed proud of her daughter, even though she couldn't keep her in a decent pair of stockings more than a day.

"Wash up, dear," was all Mama said to her slugger. "Supper's ready."

Every night was the same scene—Jodie and her mother sitting at the old kitchen table, just the two of them, talking about their day and sharing little tidbits of news about people in their small town. Sometimes Mama laughed out loud as Jodie, using arms and legs like an out-of-control octopus, told about something that happened at school or on the playground or in a baseball game.

Jodie looked nothing like her mother. She was taller than most girls her age with long, lanky legs, dark brown hair, and eyes so brown they were almost black. For sure, Jodie was a mystery to her mother. But then, Mama was an even bigger mystery to Jodie. There were so many parts of Mama she couldn't understand—the faraway look in her eyes as she gazed out the kitchen window, the soft sounds of sobbing coming from her bedroom late at night, the strange ritual of the Sunday rose. Jodie knew Mama missed her husband, the father Jodie never knew, but there seemed to be something else going on with Mama that Jodie couldn't figure out.

"Mama, you think maybe I could get my own ball and glove?" Jodie held her breath and grimaced, immediately

wishing she had not said it. She knew she shouldn't ask, but she wanted a ball and glove more than anything.

"Not anytime soon, dear," Mama said softly. "You know this time of year is bad for us. We need to save every penny to last us through the summer."

Jodie nodded, as if she understood perfectly and pretended it wasn't important anyway.

"Maybe this fall, when the gin starts up." Mama put her fork down and stared at her plate. "Maybe there'll be some extra spending money then."

"Sure, Mama," Jodie said reassuringly. But she knew there would be no extra spending money, even when her mother put in long hours down at the cotton gin during picking time. All the money she made went to paying off the bills that had piled up over the year. Even though Mama did other people's laundry and cleaned houses, it didn't nearly cover expenses. Jodie realized Mama had gotten very quiet and did not take another bite, and that made Jodie feel miserable for bringing up the ball and glove.

They hadn't always been poor. When Jodie was about three, right after her father was killed in the war in 1944, her mother worked at Flora's, the nicest and most expensive ladies' shop in town. They once lived in the house her father had bought for them on Richmond Street. Jodie didn't remember living in that house at all, but one time, Mama showed it to her. She could only imagine what it must have been like to live in such a pretty house.

Life would surely have been nice for them living on Richmond Street, but something terrible happened. Mama lost her job at Flora's, and they had to sell the pretty house. Mama never talked about the job or the reason she got fired or losing the house or anything like that. They just up and moved to a little town about thirty miles away, "to get a fresh start," as Mama put it. But there wasn't a lot of work for Mama to get started on, so last summer, when Jodie was eight, they moved back to Greenwood to this old, tired, tiny house at the end of Gaston Road. There wasn't a whole lot of work there either, and never enough money. Jodie suspected Mama just wanted to be closer to her husband's grave.

Mama never missed putting a rose on his grave every Sunday. She would sit in silence for the longest time, just staring at the headstone. This was Mama's time, and Jodie never interrupted or asked questions. She had even stopped asking questions about the secret rose, the second one that always sat on the backseat with Daddy's, the one Mama wouldn't talk about. Jodie never knew why or where her mother delivered the second rose every Sunday. It was Mama's secret.

Life for Jodie was like an old jigsaw puzzle she once got from a dressed-up Santa Claus at the men's club. There were too many pieces missing to make the whole picture come together, and it made no sense to her, so she ended up throwing the useless thing away. So many things in her life made no sense. There were too many unanswered questions—too many missing pieces—and Mama never talked about anything. Asking questions only upset Mama, and she never gave Jodie a straight answer anyway.

But, unlike the second-hand jigsaw puzzle, Jodie was finding the missing pieces. Or, rather, the missing pieces were finding her. Little by little she was learning things about her family; she simply had to keep her ears and eyes open.

One afternoon back in September Jodie had been playing jacks by herself on the deserted schoolyard, waiting on her mother to get out of a PTA meeting. Her ears perked up when she heard her mother's name. It was Mrs. Whitsitt and Mrs. Young, and they were chit-chatting about Mama's sad situation.

"It's a shame Daisy's come back," sighed Mrs. Whitsitt, pulling at her spotless, white gloves. "She won't be able to make enough to feed and clothe that child or herself."

"Oh, I know," agreed Mrs. Young. "It's a sad case."

Jodie's face got hot with anger, and she wanted to jump up in their faces and scream, "Shut up." But she didn't dare. For one, they were adults, and two, she wanted to hear what they had to say.

"If Rose hadn't made such a fuss about her working at Flora's back then," continued Mrs. Whitsitt, "she might be able to get a decent job in town. But everybody knows if 'Miss High and Mighty' is out to get you, you don't have a chance, not in this town. Lord knows, she's got more money than . . . "

Just then Mrs. Young spotted Jodie under the tree and gave Mrs. Whitsitt a hard elbow nudge. Both ladies pressed their lips together tightly and gave Jodie a sweet smile and a nod. Then they scurried away like two little squirrels with their mouths full of nuts.

Jodie's face was red hot, and her eyes filled with tears. She didn't like to hear anybody talk about her mother like that. But at least it explained the job at Flora's. Some rich lady had gotten Mama fired. But why? This opened up a whole new bunch of questions that needed to be answered. The mystery of her Mama had only grown bigger. Little did Jodie know it would take a long time before she could put together all the pieces to this puzzle that made up their lives.

One day an important piece came without warning, and it was a day Jodie would never forget.

chapter two

It was Saturday afternoon, a very hot day for the second of June, and Jodie was hunting up a baseball game. She was dragging along Frannie, who was whining about the heat and being thirsty and, "Why can't we just go inside and read a good book." Frannie hated baseball because she was too small and skinny to pick up the bat, couldn't catch a ball if it fell in her glove, and ran as slow as a knock-kneed chicken. She was hit once looking up at a ball coming straight for her face. Instead of getting out of the way or trying to catch it, she just stood and let it smack her right between the eyes, breaking her black-rimmed glasses. Boy, did she cry! And did she have a really good shiner, the envy of all the boys.

Even if Frannie hated baseball, she adored Jodie, so she followed Jodie everywhere. Though they were the same age, Jodie was a good head taller than Frannie, which made her look like a tag-along little sister. They were best friends and did everything together.

For hours, it seemed, Jodie and Frannie looked for some kids playing ball. They checked out the empty field behind the school and the alley behind Mr. White's hardware store and all the usual places where the boys played ball, but no luck. So they ducked into Pete's Drug Store, partly to get a drink of water so Frannie would hush up her fussing and partly to ask Pete where the game was. He was the only grown-up that Jodie didn't call "mister" because he couldn't stand it. Pete knew all the kids by name and almost always slipped them a piece of candy.

"Hey, Pete," said Jodie as she strolled up to the counter.

"Hey, Jodie," Pete echoed as he looked up from wiping the counter. He didn't say hey to Frannie because she had already slipped around the shelves and had her nose in a comic book. "What's up?"

"Nothin'. And that's the problem," answered Jodie. "We can't find anyone to play with."

Pete automatically got two Dixie cups and filled them with water. He didn't have to be asked on a hot day like this.

"Well, there were some boys in here awhile back." Pete slid the cups toward Jodie. "Seems like they were headed to Jeff's house. Had some bats and gloves and all with 'em. Probably got a game going on now."

Jodie made a face. Jeff lived on Hampton Avenue. She had heard her Mama call it the *uppity* part of town where the rich folks lived, and she didn't like the idea of going there. But it was baseball, and Jodie would go just about anywhere to play. So she snatched Frannie away from the book rack, said goodbye to Pete, and off they headed to find the game.

The town of Greenwood wasn't what you would call a big place, but it was big enough to be clearly divided into the rich side and the poor side. Even small Main Street had its invisible dividing line. The not-so-riches never went on the east end of the street where the jewelry store, the high-priced shoe stores, and other shops, like Flora's, were. They kept to the west end, the end of town where the small houses, the shoe factory, and most of the cotton gins were found.

As Frannie and Jodie walked to Hampton Avenue on the east side, the streets became broader with big oaks growing in straight lines down the middle of the street. The houses and the yards got bigger, much bigger. Jodie had never seen this part of town before. She held Frannie's hand as they crept along together. They were both scared of the big houses. Jodie would much rather be smacking a baseball down by the railroad or any other place on her side of town. But with no bat or ball of her own, she had little choice. They decided to walk down the alley behind the big houses until they found the game.

Finally they heard voices. They ran to a big white fence that surrounded Jeff's backyard and stopped at the gate.

"This must be the place," Jodie grinned down at Frannie.

Frannie didn't smile back or move a muscle.

"Well, c'mon." Jodie tugged at Frannie's small hand. Frannie just stood there waiting for Jodie to pull her through the gate.

Jeff had a really big, brick house with a huge backyard, a swing set, and a fort. There were only five boys gathered in the yard. Not much of a game. Jodie was disappointed, but some baseball was better than no baseball. As the two girls crept through the gate, the batter, a boy named Riley, swung and missed. He made a face at Jodie as if it were her fault.

"What do *you* want?" he said, and the others stopped and stared at her. Jodie almost backed out of the gate, but when she went to grab Frannie's arm, she realized Frannie had already found a soft spot to sit under a big oak tree and watch. Jodie was used to getting a cool reception from some of the boys. She always had to put up with a little griping from them, but her will to play was stronger than her wish to run.

"Can I hit a few?" she asked shyly.

"Aw, why don't you go play with your dolls," Riley sneered.

Jodie looked at the other boys who were still staring at her. They were all nine years old just like she was, except for Patrick, the pitcher, who was two years older. She knew if she held her ground they would let her play.

"Don't want to," Jodie answered. "Just want to hit a few."

"Yeah, go ahead," yelled Patrick. "Just get outta the way and wait your turn." He was getting impatient from waiting in the heat.

Next batter up was Jeff. He had the best bat money could buy, but he couldn't hit worth a flip. Strike three. Jeff and his shiny new bat were out. There were no jokes or name-calling, not even a snicker, because they were in his backyard, and everyone was hoping for lemonade and cookies later.

Finally, after all the boys had a turn, Jodie got to try. She grabbed one of the old bats. Though she would have loved the feel of Jeff's new bat, he was too particular about his things, so she didn't dare ask. Stepping up to the piece of cardboard that served as home plate, she took her stance.

Patrick began his wind-up. And boy, did he ever wind up! He twisted, leaned back, and lifted his leg way in the air till Jodie thought he would fall over backward. Then after all that effort, he threw a ball that came surprisingly right toward her bat. *Wham!* Jodie whacked that ball clean over the fence into the next yard. Everybody's mouth dropped open.

"Shouldn't hit it so hard!" yelled Jeff. "Now look what you've done."

"You gotta go get it," sneered Riley. And they all stood, gloves on hips, and stared at Jodie.

"Okay, okay," grumbled Jodie as she threw down the bat. Even though she hated having to get the ball back, she was still proud of the way it sailed over that fence. She started for the gate, then turned and asked, "Who lives there anyway?"

Jeff looked at the other boys and then at Jodie in disbelief.

"What do you mean, *who lives there?*" he jeered. "You should know; she's your aunt."

Jodie gasped so hard she got dizzy and almost fell down. Unable to believe what she had just heard, she stopped dead still and stared at the faces around her. The other boys were nodding their heads in agreement. Everyone seemed to know she had an aunt who lived in the big house next door. Everyone, that is, but Jodie. *How could this be? Why hadn't her mother told her she had an aunt? An aunt living on Hampton Avenue? Who was this person? This just could not be true!*

Jodie hoped her face didn't show what she was feeling inside. She pretended not to be surprised and acted as though she knew all along, but it was too late. And as kids will do to other kids, they couldn't help but rub it in.

18

"You mean," Jeff cocked his head to one side and sneered at Jodie. "You didn't know Miss Parker was your aunt? My mama said she was your mama's sister. I heard Mama tell Mrs. Finney that your mama and your Aunt Rose don't even talk to each other."

He had said *Aunt Rose* like it was a dirty name, and all the boys snickered.

"Yeah," added Patrick. "I heard your mama can't work at that dress store or any other place in town 'cause Miss Parker won't hear of it."

Jodie's head was spinning from all the confusion. Fighting back tears that were hot behind her eyes, she wheeled away from the boys and headed for the back gate. She would have to ask Mama about all this, but right now, she had to get that ball.

Jodie looked to Frannie for help. She nodded her head toward the gate. But Frannie didn't budge. She motioned with her arm in an urgent gesture to *get up and come on*, but Frannie still sat and stared at her. Frannie wasn't about to sneak into the backyard of some strange, rich lady. Not even for her very best friend.

Frustrated, Jodie stomped out the gate to Jeff's backyard and down the alley till she was next door. She would face the danger all alone. Who needed them anyway? After all, they said the lady who lived in the big white house was her aunt. Jodie stopped and faced the new gate. All the more reason to be fearful.

She gulped, straightened her cap, slowly put her hands on the gate, and gave a little push. It hung on the grass, and she had to lift it up and push really hard just to make enough room to squeeze through. Once inside, she gasped at what she saw. It was such a beautiful sight it actually took her breath away. Pretty white wicker chairs sat on a brick patio. A lattice-work archway, covered with vines intertwined with flowers, stood at one end. And a million rose bushes, it seemed, lined the yard. Beautiful pinks and reds and whites.

"Oh my," Jodie whispered to herself. All she could do was stare at the beautiful sight. She had never seen such a pretty yard in her whole life. She didn't know how long she had been standing there when she remembered why she had come.

"Have to get that stupid ball," she said to herself. But her feet were glued in fear to the spot where she was standing. Her eyes searched frantically for the small white ball. Where was that ball? Nowhere in sight.

So she took a few steps onto the soft, thick grass and peeked around the gate. No ball. But what she did see took her breath again, this time from fright not beauty. Trembling, she froze in place.

It *was* her mother.

At least she thought so at first. The woman was bending over the rose bushes and had not seen Jodie. At least Jodie didn't think so. Wanting to turn and run, she couldn't take her eyes off the lady. Jodie watched as the woman straightened and turned to the side. It was her mother, in a slightly bigger body with darker hair that was pulled up in a bun on top of her head.

Jodie stared, unable to believe what she saw. Suddenly, the lady turned to Jodie, making Jodie jump with surprise. Her blue eyes pierced right through the girl. These, too, looked like her mother's except they weren't warm and loving, but cold and staring instead, like cubes of blue ice.

"This what you're looking for?" the lady asked in a soft but harsh voice. She held out her hand with the baseball in it.

Jodie could only nod.

"Well, speak up," she scolded. "You can talk, can't you?"

Jodie nodded again. Then shook her head and cleared her throat.

"Yes, ma'am," Jodie managed to squeak out.

"Then here," the lady offered the ball. "Come get it."

Jodie stepped lightly on the soft grass to where Miss Parker stood and reached for the ball. For a few seconds, their hands met on the small object. Miss Parker did not let go but bent down and looked Jodie hard in the face. Jodie thought she was in for the scolding of her life.

"Sorry, miss," whispered Jodie, thinking the lady was waiting for an apology. But Miss Parker didn't seem to hear. She just stared at Jodie in the strangest way, and for the longest time, until Jodie almost let go of the ball to run away.

Then, very quickly, Miss Parker let Jodie take the ball, turned around, and headed for the house. She did not yell or tell her to get out or anything. She just walked away.

Jodie was stunned. She had never met anyone like Miss Parker before, so much like her mother, and yet so strange and unfriendly. *Get out* was all Jodie could think to do. *Get out and get home!* She wanted to know more about this aunt she had never met. She wanted to see the soft, warm eyes of her mother. She needed a hug. Right then and there, she promised never to come here again.

That night at supper Jodie was especially quiet. This behavior was so unusual that Mama reached over to feel her forehead.

"You feeling all right, hon'?" Mama asked as she rubbed Jodie's face.

"Yes, ma'am," she muttered.

"Well, you don't feel warm, but you're acting awfully strange."

Jodie sat quietly. She was thinking about all the strange things that had happened that afternoon. Then suddenly she blurted out, "Mama, do you really have a sister?"

Mama dropped her fork. Her look of concern turned immediately to one of shock, and her face turned white. Staring at her daughter for several seconds as if she couldn't believe what she had just heard, Mama picked up her plate and took it to the sink where she began to wash it in silence.

Jodie thought her mother didn't hear her, so she tried again.

"Mama," she began. "Do you . . ."

"Yes," Mama interrupted and turned to face her daughter. Looking at Jodie for a few seconds, Mama then came back to the table and sat down. She put her fragile hand on top of Jodie's.

"Rose Parker is my sister," Mama admitted. Jodie could feel her mother's hand shaking. "She's your aunt."

"But, Mama," Jodie asked. "How come I've never met her? How come she doesn't visit us?"

Mama took a deep breath and shook her head.

"It's hard to explain," she sighed. "You'll understand when you're older."

Mama leaned over and kissed Jodie on the forehead.

"I love you," was all she said before gathering the rest of the dishes.

Jodie's head was still swimming. She had never known very much about her family. Her father had been killed in the war, and she had seen pictures of her grandparents. They were all buried in the old cemetery on Cedar Hill. She guessed her grandparents must have been rich people a long time ago because their headstone was about the biggest one in the whole place. But whenever she asked Mama about them, Mama only cried and said, "We'll talk about it later."

And now, out of nowhere, there was an aunt, an aunt Jodie had never in her life heard about. This very same person, her mother's own sister, had caused Mama to lose her good job. This was surely a family mystery, the biggest, and everybody knows family secrets run very deep and very quiet. Jodie didn't ask her mother any more questions. She would be patient. Jodie was sure that one day, like Mama said, when she was older, she would know and better understand the secrets. Time always reveals the truth, and that's scary.

chapter three

Jodie was awakened by the soft pecking of raindrops on her window. She raised her head to watch the tiny beads of water hit the glass and roll in squiggly lines down the window pane. It was Sunday. And Jodie knew Mama would be calling soon. Jodie could smell the pancakes cooking on the griddle, and that alone was worth getting out of her warm, cozy bed. She swung her legs off the side of the bed and searched the floor with her toes for the pair of socks she had kicked off the night before.

Yawning and stretching, she slipped the dirty socks on her cold feet, and headed for the kitchen. As she shuffled silently into the doorway of the small room, Mama yelled, "Jodie dear, time to get up!"

"Okay, Mama," Jodie said and giggled as Mama jumped in surprise.

"I should've known you'd be up." Mama smiled as she flipped a big, golden-brown pancake onto a plate. "The smell of good hotcakes could raise you from the dead."

"Mm-m-m-m." Jodie sniffed the steam rising from her plate. "You're right about that."

"Well, we don't have much time to get to church this morning," warned Mama. "I guess I fell back to sleep. We gotta get a move on."

Mama had been doing that a lot lately. She seemed to be tired all the time, taking naps in the afternoon, falling asleep at the oddest times, oversleeping in the mornings. Jodie knew her mother worked awfully hard, yet she had never seen her so tired before. This behavior puzzled Jodie.

They made up for lost time by leaving the dirty dishes in the sink and the beds unmade, something Mama never did, and they dressed as quickly as possible. Jodie was still twisting and grabbing at the back of her dress, trying to button those stupid buttons right between her shoulder blades, as she headed out the door. The sash of her dress was flowing behind her, and her shoes were unbuckled.

"Oh, Jodie," Mama called from behind the steering wheel. "Let me help you."

"No, Mama," Jodie said through clenched teeth, still wrestling with the back of her dress. "You just get this old car cranked up. You know how ornery it can be."

Mama was pumping on the gas pedal and twisting the key as the old motor grinded. She jiggled the gear stick, pumped again, and squeezed the key with all her might. It was the same routine every day. You'd think the old car had a mind of its own, determined not to kick over without first wearing out Mama.

"Get goin', you old mule!" Jodie fussed and hit the dashboard.

The motor gave a little sputter, choked, and died. Mama started her routine again. This time the worn-out engine kicked in, shaking as if it had a terrible chill.

"Just needs a good talking to." Jodie grinned as the stubborn car jerked out of the driveway onto the dirt road. Mama looked over at her daughter and stifled a chuckle.

"Oh, Jodie, hon'." Mama smiled and shook her head. Jodie's dress was all bunched up in the back where she had fastened the buttons in the wrong buttonholes. One sash was hung in the crooked opening of her dress while the other one draped over the car seat. Her shoes, which had never been buckled, were on the wrong feet.

"Better to be on time than dressed right," Jodie said. "The Lord doesn't care too much about clothes, but He sure hates it when people are late."

Jodie knew no matter how pressed for time they were Mama would not forget about the Sunday rose. Sneaking a peek in the backseat, Jodie saw that, sure enough, there were two deep red roses beside Mama's old, crumpled umbrella. Jodie quit asking Mama about the *secret rose* years ago, just because she got tired of hearing the same old answer, "You'll understand when you're older." Jodie figured she'd be ninety-nine years old and still not know what Mama did with the rose each Sunday. So she just waited patiently as Mama pulled the car over to the curb.

The rain had stopped by now, so Mama left the umbrella on the seat. She picked up the beautiful rose and headed down the street. Soon Mama disappeared around the corner hidden by a tall wooden fence.

Jodie hummed a few bars of "O When the Saints Come Marching In," tried smoothing down her rain-soaked hair, and tugged at her dress that was too tight because it was all twisted up in the back.

In a few minutes, Mama's slight figure appeared from around the corner, and they were soon off again toward church, no questions asked, no explanations given.

Church was a small building that held just enough people to be considered a *real* church. Not like the huge Presbyterian church at the end of Main Street where most all the rich people went. Small though it was, Mama and Jodie liked their little church just fine. Nobody stared at their clothes or whispered about them from the pew behind, loud enough to be heard *accidentally*, or rolled their eyes at how much money Mama put in the offering plate or, rather, didn't put in. And there was always someone to help them get the car started if it didn't want to go home or change a flat tire if they'd picked up a nail on the way there. Mama and Jodie felt right at home and rarely ever missed a service.

Just inside the door Jodie saw three boys from her class at school. They were talking excitedly about something, and, of course, Jodie had to know.

"Yeah, next Saturday," Tim was saying. "You can bet I'll be there."

"Me too," added Buster. "Hey, how about coming over to my house to practice?"

"Hey, Tim," Jodie interrupted. "Hey, Buster, Walt. What's up?"

"The men's club is starting a little league team," Walt answered. "Try-outs are this Saturday."

"Oh yeah?" said Jodie a little too calmly. "Where are the try-outs?"

Just then the organ blasted the little room with the first chords of the opening hymn. Jodie's mother cut off her conversation with Mrs. Willis and took Jodie by the arm, pulling at her newly-tied sash and pressing down her collar. Jodie didn't see why all the members were scurrying so fast to get to their pews. The same people had sat in the same pew for the past fifty years, so there was certainly no danger in losing your seat.

Jodie tried hard to listen to Brother Stevens' message, but her mind kept jumping from the temptations of the devil to baseball. A little league! Boy, this little town was moving up! They'd never had a real team for kids. Visions of a storehouse of bats, balls, and gloves popped into Jodie's head. Maybe they would let her take some equipment home, just to practice. Real games with real umpires. She'd have to teach her Mama to yell, "Kill the ump!" if Jodie ever got called out on a slide. Would there be uniforms? Yes, real honest-to-goodness uniforms—with shoes! Jodie got herself so excited just thinking about it she almost squealed out loud.

After the last *amen*, Jodie hurried to find the boys and ask where the try-outs would be held. But Mama stopped her to talk with Mrs. Turner who had three kids and one on the way and wondered if Jodie might do a little baby-sitting for her. Jodie eyed the two little girls and their three-year-old brother who had been picking at each other and fidgeting all during the service and thought she'd rather eat pig slop than keep those kids. But she smiled sweetly at Mrs. Turner and answered politely how wonderful that would be. Jodie knew any chance of making a little money to help Mama could not be passed up.

By the time Mama and Jodie got to the front door Jodie's friends were nowhere in sight. *Oh well*, she thought, she could find out later. She made a mental list of all the things she needed to do before Saturday—practice her pitching, especially her curve ball, run a few laps every day, do a few push-ups, and practice, practice, practice.

Next morning Jodie was up, dressed, had a pan of biscuits in the oven, and was sorting two large bundles of laundry left on their porch by Mr. Morgan, all before her mother woke up. Jodie picked lightly through the clothes with the fingertips of one hand and held her nose with the other. Mr. Morgan was a butcher, and his aprons were always nasty. She couldn't stand to touch them. On top of that, he had seven kids who were wild as tomcats because their mother couldn't keep up with them. Mrs. Morgan was a sickly woman who always had headaches. With all those kids, who wouldn't have headaches? Their clothes looked like they wallowed in a pig sty and smelled like it, too.

Just as Jodie was taking the biscuits out of the oven, steaming hot and smelling delicious, she heard her mother shuffling to the bathroom. Mama was having a coughing fit, and Jodie set the biscuits down quickly to see about her.

"Just a little dust," Mama explained.

Jodie wasn't convinced, but she didn't push her mother. She knew Mama would never go back to bed even if she needed to.

"My stars, dear!" Mama exclaimed when she entered the tiny kitchen. "You've been busy this morning."

Jodie beamed proudly and poured her mother a glass of juice.

"No time to waste," Jodie answered. "Got lots to do."

Then Jodie told Mama about the little league and the try-outs on Saturday and how she needed to practice this and that and so on and so on. She was spewing words out like lava from a volcano; Mama was listening and smiling lovingly.

Jodie was busy all day helping Mama with the laundry. Sometimes Mama let Jodie iron things that were easy, like pillowcases or handkerchiefs, but mostly she washed, hung the clothes on the line, and folded. Monday was always the busiest day for doing laundry, but today the work seemed endless. Jodie was so antsy to get outside and practice, practice, practice. But every time she thought she had folded the last blouse, Mama would drop a new bundle of clothes on the kitchen floor, and they'd start all over again.

Jodie felt like screaming or crying or just stomping out the door. Why couldn't these people do their own laundry? But then she looked at her mother who was so thin and pale, who never stopped to rest or ever uttered a word of complaint, and it made her feel guilty for being such a whiner.

Mama seemed to read her mind.

"We'll be finished soon enough, hon," she said softly. "You know, Jodie, we ought to be thankful there's so much work to be done."

Jodie knew Mama was right. They were sure enough poor, but without this laundry, they wouldn't even have money for food. So Jodie put her mind to the work as best she could and hoped there'd be time left for a little baseball.

By Thursday things weren't looking too good. Nothing had turned out like she'd planned. She had not gotten in one minute of practice, what with all the laundry to be done and houses to be cleaned and baby-sitting Mrs. Turner's kids while she went to the doctor to find out she was not only having another one but twins. Jodie was beside herself!

"Jodie, dear," her mother said as they sat down for breakfast. "You really don't need to worry about practicing so much. You're very good at baseball already. You'll do fine at try-outs."

"Oh, no, Mama," Jodie shook her head. She had a very worried look on her face. "There'll be lots of boys trying out. Older boys who can hit like a firecracker and throw the fastest pitch you ever saw. I *gotta* practice."

"Well, I tell you what," Mama reached over and patted Jodie's hand. "You can have all afternoon. I promise."

Jodie beamed.

Speeding through the few chores she had to do like a steam engine, she finally got the okay from Mama, and she ran out of the house like it was on fire. She had to find Frannie and then a ball game.

Frannie was easy to find, but the game was a different story. The two friends looked everywhere for some kids, any kids, playing baseball. Even Pete at the drug store was no help.

"Try Jeff's house," Pete suggested. "There's usually a group of kids who like to play there." He leaned over the counter and winked at Jodie and Frannie. "I hear his mama makes good lemonade and cookies."

They looked at each other and frowned. No way would they go back to Jeff's house. Not for a million dollars or even a new ball and glove.

So the two girls raced back to Jodie's house. They would just have to make do with what they could find. Jodie came out of her house with an old broom handle. Frannie looked at it and just shook her head.

"What?" Jodie snapped at Frannie. "It'll do. You'll see."

"So where are you going to get a ball?" asked Frannie.

Jodie thought a minute; then she grabbed Frannie by the hand and took off. They ran across the field by Jodie's house to a big tree. Catching her breath, Jodie said, "These. We'll use these."

"What are they?" Frannie asked looking at the strange green balls. They looked like giant, green oranges.

"Mama calls them goose-apples," Jodie answered. "I don't know what they are, *exactly*, but they'll do for baseballs."

So they gathered as many goose-apples as they could hold and made their way back to Jodie's yard.

By dusk, Jodie had seen another wasted day go by without good practice. Not only was Frannie a terrible pitcher, but if Jodie did manage to whack the goose-apple, it would shatter into a jillion pieces. It didn't take long to go through the whole bunch.

Jodie went to bed tired and frustrated and determined to find a way to practice on the one day left before try-outs. She put those thoughts into a prayer that night before she closed her

eyes. Not a real nice prayer like she normally said, thanking God for all His many blessings, more like "Oh, Lord, please don't let it rain and please, *please*, find me a baseball game tomorrow. I've got to practice." But, whether it was a nice prayer or not, it got answered.

chapter four

Friday morning was a beautiful day. Jodie was up bright and early to get started on any jobs her mother had for her. She began getting breakfast ready like she had done every morning since school had been out. Her mother seemed to stay in bed later and later each morning.

"Jodie, hon'," she called from her bedroom. "Go ahead and eat breakfast. Don't wait on me this morning."

Jodie went to her mother's bedroom door. Mama was still lying in the bed, coughing something awful.

"Mama, you all right?" asked Jodie.

"Yes, dear, yes," Mama caught her breath. "You go on outside today and get some practicing in. You deserve a day off."

Jodie would have jumped up and down and whooped with joy, but something about the way her mother looked and sounded made her feet stick solidly to the floor.

"Mama," Jodie stepped closer to Mama's bed. "You *sure* you're all right?"

"I'm tired, that's all," Mama said. "A little extra sleep will help."

Jodie didn't budge from her mother's bed.

Mama pretended to be annoyed.

"Now shoo," Mama insisted, waving her hand. "Go on. I'll be up in a few minutes. Get going."

She smiled and pointed her finger at Jodie. "Remember practice, practice, practice."

Jodie smiled back and headed for the door. Halfway down the hall to the kitchen, she stopped and ran back to tell Mama she'd be back in time to fix lunch. But Mama had already drifted back to sleep. Jodie tiptoed out of the house. She was worried about her mother, but right now she had to get down to business.

The first order of business was to round up Frannie. Jodie found her friend still sitting at the breakfast table, and no matter how impatient Jodie appeared, there was no moving her little friend from that table until Frannie's mother gave the okay. After a few more pecks with her fork, Frannie was finally freed. Off the two ran to the baseball field beside the old cotton warehouse. That's when the second part of Jodie's prayer was answered.

A group of boys was just forming teams to start a game. Most of the boys were Jodie's age, some were older. She guessed they would all be trying out for the little league the next day. Jodie's spine tingled with excitement. She loved a real game.

"C'mon," Jodie nudged Frannie gently. "Don't act too eager."

Frannie looked at Jodie through her big-rimmed glasses and sighed. She was anything but eager, and it showed. She would much rather be home reading her mother's new *McCall's* magazine.

"Boys are so stingy when it comes to baseball," Jodie chattered on. "They think it was invented just for them or something." She shook her head and continued walking slowly toward the baseball field.

Then it happened. THUD! Something hit Jodie on the back between the shoulders so hard she lost her balance. She was falling right for the ground, face first, and dragging poor little Frannie down with her.

Somehow Jodie managed to let go of Frannie's hand and catch herself before her face smashed in the dirt. There was laughter behind her, and Jodie could feel her face get hot and red.

She jumped up and whirled around to see Tommy the Terrible and two of his friends, Ollie and Nick. He had smacked her hard on the back with his baseball, and now they were pointing at her and holding their sides, as if her fall had been side-splitting funny.

Then Tommy stopped laughing, walked over to Jodie, and breathed in her face.

"What're you doing here?" he sneered.

Jodie wanted to yell in his face to go eat a frog, but she was so angry her jaws just clenched tightly together. She could feel Frannie behind her shaking like a scared rabbit.

"Get outta here!" he snapped. "Girls don't play baseball. And we gotta practice for the try-outs tomorrow. We don't have time to be messing with you. Go home, or we'll really let you have it."

The other two boys echoed Tommy's warning. Jodie could feel Frannie tugging at the back of her shirt. She would love to snatch up Frannie, bolt, and run home, but she wasn't moving. This was much too important. It was worth risking a black eye or worse.

"Oh *yeah*?" Jodie snapped back. "Well, for your information, I gotta practice, too."

Tommy looked back over his shoulder at his friends. He smirked that ugly, nasty smirk and turned back to her.

"What do you think?" Tommy glared at her. "That *you're* gonna try out for *our* little league team?" He looked around at his friends again. "Not a chance. You think they'd let a girl play on a boys' team?"

All three friends let out a loud, fake laugh. Jodie could feel her face get hot and red again. The anger boiled up inside till she thought she would pop right then and there like an over-blown balloon.

"You're lying!" Jodie screamed. "You'll see. I can play just as good as you."

Tommy leaned back and folded his arms on his chest. He really enjoyed seeing Jodie fly off the handle. He loved watching the look on her face as the bad news sunk in.

"Hey," he said smugly. "I didn't make the rules. I'm just telling you. Girls aren't allowed on this team. Go ask anyone."

Jodie looked at each boy squarely in the face. She could see the mock innocence and fake remorse for her, but she could also see that it was the truth. She was so stunned she could hardly breathe. It was all she could do to keep the tears from bursting from her eyes. Thank goodness the game started, and Tommy and his friends took off to join.

When they were completely out of sight, Jodie plopped down right there in the dirt. Frannie sat in the dirt, too, scooted close beside her friend, and patted her as she sobbed. Jodie was heartbroken. She had never wanted anything so much in her life, and now it had been snatched out of her reach. It wasn't *fair*. It just wasn't fair. Boys got to do everything, even if they weren't half as good as she was.

She felt as if her world had just ended. As she and Frannie shuffled back home, the wheels of Jodie's mind began to turn. There had to be a way to get on that team. She would just have to sit down and figure out what to do. By the time Saturday morning dawned, she had done just that.

chapter five

It was unusually hot for nine o'clock in the morning. Tiny sweat beads formed at Jodie's temples and slowly inched down her cheeks. Maybe she was just nervous. Or maybe it was all those clothes she had on.

There she was, sitting at the end of the bench on the edge of the baseball field, hunched down and still as a statue. As she waited for her name to be called, she was afraid to look up or side-to-side or move a muscle. She had thought of a plan. Whether it would work was another thing, and she'd soon find out. So far, nobody discovered her secret. She tried to stay quiet, invisible, completely unnoticed, especially by Tommy the Terrible and his buddies.

Jodie glanced up at the stands behind her. No Frannie. Jodie missed her little friend, even if Frannie usually read a book instead of watch Jodie play. They had both decided it was best if she didn't show up. It might spoil the plan.

The plan had been all Jodie's idea. And this was it. Today, Jodie was a boy.

She had gotten up very early, dressed in her usual T-shirt and shorts, kissed her mother good-by, and headed for the try-outs.

"Are you going to wear those old shoes?" Her mother had noticed that Jodie was wearing her tennis shoes from last year that had holes in both toes.

"Oh, these?" Jodie looked down as if she had forgotten what she had put on her feet. Truth was, the shoes were killing her toes, but they were the only boy-looking shoes she owned. "Yes, ma'am. They're my lucky ones."

Barely hearing her mother say, "Good luck" as she bounded out the door, Jodie headed straight for Frannie's.

Frannie was no good when it came to helping Jodie practice. She thought of how terrible Frannie was at pitching goose-apples and how awkward she looked when she tried to run. Jodie could see Frannie running in circles trying to catch big chunks of their funny, green "baseballs" when Jodie had smacked it into a thousand pieces. But, as useless as Frannie was in practice, she outdid herself on her part of the plan. Jodie didn't know her little friend could be so sneaky.

Frannie was waiting on her back porch. Their first task was to sneak past Frannie's mother, an almost impossible thing to do. She was one of those mothers who has eyes in the back of her head and ears like radars. But luck was with them so far. Frannie's mother was elbow-deep in a bowl of batter with bacon sizzling in the skillet and a pot of water starting to boil. She was much too busy to see two little girls scurry past the kitchen door.

Once inside Frannie's room, Jodie started to squeal with delight when Frannie slapped her hand over Jodie's mouth. In a small bed by the wall, Frannie's older sister, Betty Jean, was still sleeping, and they certainly couldn't take a chance on her waking up and tattling on them. But Jodie was so excited she could hardly keep from giggling out loud.

Frannie had come through with her half of the plan. There on the bed were a pair of boy's jeans, a long-sleeved T-shirt, and a ball cap. They belonged to her twelve-year-old brother, Ralph, who was, like Frannie, small for his age. Everything would fit Jodie to a tee.

Jodie quickly exchanged her shorts for the jeans. Just as she reached for the shirt, there was a rustle in the direction of Betty Jean's bed. Frannie and Jodie froze. They held their breaths as Betty Jean rolled over, pulled the covers up to her ears, and let out a terrible snort. She had not opened her eyes. Both girls let out a sigh of relief.

Frannie waved her hands at Jodie as if to say, "Hurry up, hurry up!" She knew her mother would be calling everybody for breakfast any minute. Jodie jerked the long-sleeved shirt over her own T-shirt to save time. She wanted as little of her skin to show as possible. Then Frannie pointed to Jodie's head, motioned her to sit on the floor, and produced a rubber band from around her wrist. Good ole Frannie! She thought of everything.

Just as Frannie finished wadding Jodie's hair in a ball on top of her head, they were startled by the loud, piercing voice of Frannie's mother.

Betty Jean rolled over again. Frannie and Jodie panicked. Jodie had to get out and quick!

Frannie slammed the ball cap on Jodie's head and pushed her with both hands toward the window. It was already half-open, so Frannie gave it a good shove as Jodie swung both legs over the sill and dropped to the ground.

"What's going on?" Jodie could hear Betty Jean say in a drowsy voice. But she didn't wait around to hear Frannie's cool explanation, something about bugs and wind and she would just shut the window because it was time for breakfast. Smiling, Jodie sneaked through the bushes and dashed across the yard. She was lucky to have a good friend like Frannie.

Jodie pulled at her ball cap for the ninety-ninth time. She kept it low over her face as she waited for the try-outs to start. If they ever *would* start. It seemed like hours since she had signed the list as Joe Miller. The waiting was making her all fidgety and sweaty. Her stomach felt like it was tied in a huge knot. Actually, she thought she might throw up, right there in front of the whole world. She wasn't at all sure if she could even hold a bat in this condition.

And what a lot of bats there were! The sight of all those baseball bats lying in a row on the ground had taken her breath away. Jodie could picture herself propping one of them on her shoulder and strutting home with it to practice. She was deep in daydreams of practicing with a real ball and hitting homers with every swing when a loud voice shook her back to reality.

". . . and you will each get a turn a bat," the voice was saying. It was Mr. Cooper, who was a mailman most of the time but now was the coach of the little league team. He explained all about the team and what each boy would need to do if he made the cut. The word *boy* made Jodie's stomach knot up again, and she had to fight back the urge to get sick. She was glad she had not eaten the oatmeal and biscuits Mama made for breakfast.

Mr. Cooper began assigning boys to positions on the field. Jodie held her breath until enough boys were picked, and then she let out a sigh of relief.

Feeling like she was stuck to the bench in fear, she wiped her hands on her borrowed jeans for the hundredth time. How could she hold a bat with these sweaty, trembling hands?

The first boy was called to bat. Everything was just a blur to Jodie. She was so nervous she could hardly watch him. He swung once. Strike one. He swung again. Strike two. This got Jodie's attention. She realized the boy was Tommy the Terrible's friend, Nick. Although he had seemed really scary yesterday, he didn't look so tough now. He looked more like a whipped dog as he swung, strike three, and left the plate with his head down and his feet dragging.

Jodie watched a second boy step to the plate. Swing, foul ball, swing, strike two, swing, pop fly caught by the pitcher. Then a third boy tried with just about the same results.

What is wrong with these boys? Jodie thought to herself. They couldn't hit worth a flip. She felt her confidence returning. *Just give me a bat. I'll show you who needs to be on this team.*

Then Mr. Cooper called, "Tommy White."

Fear struck. Her body tensed. Her skin got all goose-bumpy. Tommy the Terrible walked past her on his way to pick up a bat. She hunched down as low as she could so he wouldn't recognize her. She remembered yesterday, the hard hit on the back that, in fact, created a bruise and the warning he and his friends had given her. If they found out what she was doing, they'd rip her apart. Suddenly, her courage was gone.

This is not a good plan at all, Jodie thought to herself. She wanted to be on the little league team more than anything. She wanted to use their bats and balls. She wanted to wear a baseball uniform. But now she began to think of a way to escape. Preparing to make a run for the gate, she heard a strange name.

41

"Joe Miller," called Mr. Cooper in a booming voice.

No one got up. No one answered.

Mr. Cooper looked around and up and down the bench.

"Joe Miller," he repeated even louder.

Jodie then realized he was calling her. *She* was Joe Miller. But she did not move; she was frozen to the bench. Why hadn't she made a run for it sooner? Sitting perfectly still with her head down, she hoped Mr. Cooper would forget about Joe Miller.

Everything came to a standstill. It seemed as if the world had stopped, waiting for her to answer. There wasn't a sound except for the ringing in Jodie's ears. *Go to the next name. Please go to the next name*, was all Jodie could think.

Then Jodie saw a pair of old brown wing-tips appear on the ground directly in front of her. She slowly peered up from under the ball cap. It was Mr. Cooper, clipboard in hand and whistle around his neck, looking down at her.

"Aren't you Joe Miller?" he asked.

Jodie could only nod her head.

"It's your turn, son," he added. "Grab a bat and let's go."

Somehow Jodie managed to lift herself off the bench. Making her way slowly over to the row of bats, she picked up the closest one. She passed Tommy the Terrible on her way to the plate, but he seemed to look right through her. While she had been busy thinking of a way to get away, Tommy had struck out. He was still reeling from the shock of it and, thank the Lord, did not notice her.

Jodie took a deep breath and stepped up to the plate. One of the dads was pitching, and she nodded to him when she felt comfortable with her stance. The bat felt good in her hands. It seemed to fill her with power, like a wave of heat going through her body. The fear melted away. There was no crowd, no Tommy the Terrible, no snickering boys. Just herself, the bat, and that little white ball coming her way. This was what she lived for, and she gave it all she had.

And all she had sent that little ball sailing over the baseball field, above the heads of the boys in the outfield with their mouths open, and clean over the fence. The only sound that could be heard was the loud thud it made as it banged the side of the old cotton warehouse. At first everyone was too stunned to utter a sound. Then the air was filled with loud whoops and yells: the fuel to Jodie's pumping legs as she sped to first base. With a hit like that she didn't need to run, but it felt good.

So good she raced with all her might, touched first, rounded second, and flew through third while the cheers got louder and louder. Jodie was on top of the world.

It was in the split second before reaching home plate that Jodie decided to go all out, just for show. If they wanted to see her best, then she would give it to them. She took a giant leap and slid on her stomach into home plate. A thick cloud of dust and the cheers of the crowd both engulfed her, nearly smothering her. Totally out of breath, Jodie lay on the ground, panting with joy. She felt she could absolutely explode with pride. She *would* make the team; there could be no doubt. She had shown all of them who was best. The coach, the other dads, the boys, even the mothers, and friends in the bleachers, had all cheered for her.

But in the few seconds it took for the dust to settle and Jodie to pull herself to her feet, the world came to a screeching halt. The cheering that had been ringing in her ears as she rounded the bases had suddenly stopped, and she realized there was dead silence. She looked at all the faces surrounding her. All the boys, Mr. Cooper, and the dads were looking at her as if she had grown a second head.

What's going on here? Jodie thought to herself, confused. There should be slaps on the back, words of congratulations, but there were only shocked looks and gaping mouths.

Then, to her horror, Jodie saw the reason for the sudden silence. Her ball cap was lying on the ground at her feet. With a shaking hand, she slowly inched her fingers to the neck of her T-shirt. She nervously stretched the finger-tips to the back of her neck, and her worst nightmare came true. There, hanging in soft curls, was her hair for everyone to see.

The secret was out. What would they do to her? She could make a break for it, but she was outnumbered. It was no use.

She was caught. She looked at Mr. Cooper with eyes begging for mercy. He merely looked back at her in disbelief.

After what seemed like an eternity, Mr. Cooper finally spoke up.

'This is quite a surprise, I must say," he flipped his cap up with one hand and gave his head a scratch. "I guess you're not Joe Miller."

"No, sir," Jodie confessed, looking at the ground.

"I can't tell you how sorry that makes me," he continued. "A whole truckload of sorry, that's for sure."

Mr. Cooper looked around at the others straining to hear what was being said. He put his arm around Jodie's shoulder and walked her over to the fence out of listening range. There, he squatted down to her level and spoke softer.

"I'll be honest with you, dear," Mr. Cooper sounded very sincere. "I've never seen a little leaguer crack a ball the way you did. Why-y-y, I was already seeing the championship trophy in our hands." He chuckled, then saw Jodie's stricken look and got serious again.

"You know there are rules," Mr. Cooper cleared his throat and used his sleeve to wipe the sweat off his forehead. This conversation was not easy for him. "This team is for boys. We just *can't* let a girl play on a boys' team. Why-y-y, what would the other teams think? Huh? And what would the parents say? And the boys . . . what about the other boys on the team? Huh?"

Jodie was trembling from head to toe. She could not look Mr. Cooper in the face nor could she stop the tears from rolling down her face.

"Yes – sir- ree, that was the best doggone hit I ever did see," said Mr. Cooper, trying to make her feel better. "But there's no question about it. A girl can't be on a boys' team." Mr. Cooper shook his head. "No. It's just not heard of. I'm sorry, dear, but that's the way things are."

"*Plea-ea-se,* Mr. Cooper," Jodie begged in a sobbing voice. "Please let me play. I'll do anything you say. I'll practice every day. I won't fuss with the boys or start a fight or anything. Just please let me try it."

It was almost more than Mr. Cooper could take. Seeing a little girl so heartbroken, the tear-stained face, the soft, pleading voice, made him choke on the words he had to say.

"Aw, sweetheart," he reached down and patted her shoulder. "Don't take it so hard. There's nothing anybody can do. That's just the way things are."

Mr. Cooper was about to bawl himself, so he broke away from Jodie, turned, and walked away quickly.

Jodie knew it was no use. What had seemed to be the most wonderful moment in her whole life turned out to be the end of all her dreams and wishes. She had to get away from here, from these horrible people. Through tear-blurred eyes, she found the gate and headed for it. She knew everyone was still staring at her, but she didn't run. Their stares could burn a hole in her back for all she cared. She was too drained to do anything more than slowly drag her feet down the road and out of sight.

With each step Jodie's disappointment turned into anger. She hated the whole world. She hated boys. She hated baseball. She hated that rock on the road, and she gave it a terrific kick, sending it flying high through the air. Then she hopped and yelped in pain, holding her toe because her shoes were still too tight and kicking the rock had only made it hurt worse. She hated these shoes. In a fit of rage she yanked off one shoe and threw it with all her might. Hopping on the shoeless foot, she yanked the other one off and did the same. The rock and the shoes were nowhere to be seen, but Jodie didn't care. She continued to stomp down the road in a terrible, boiling anger.

Although she knew deep down in her heart she didn't mean it, she hated Frannie for the broken rubber band, and she hated Frannie's brother for his cap that flew off. She was so mad she was even mad at her mother, but she didn't know exactly why. Mama should've known better than to have a girl: better not to have had a baby at all. And, worst of all, she was mad at God. Nobody should be mad at God, Jodie knew, but she couldn't help it. God should have made her a boy. It wasn't fair. It just wasn't fair.

When Jodie reached her front yard, Mama was busy hanging out clothes on the line. She dropped the blouse in her hand out of sheer shock at the sight of her daughter. There stood Jodie—shoeless, hair tangled, covered in dust from head to toe, and wearing someone else's clothes.

"Good Lord, Jodie!" her mother exclaimed as she ran toward her. "What's happened? What are these clothes? What happened to your shoes?" Like mamas do, she was checking out Jodie, looking for cuts and bruises and working herself up into a terrible fuss. Not until she cupped Jodie's face in her hands did she see the evidence of the tears.

"What is it?" Mama almost shrieked. "What's happened, baby?"

Jodie looked at her mother, and the tears swelled up again. She grabbed her mother around the waist and buried her head in Mama's dress. Jodie cried long and hard until she could cry no longer. Then she and Mama sat on the porch steps, and, with her head in Mama's lap, Jodie let her mother stroke her hair as she spilled all the details of the past few hours. Jodie was lucky her mother was a good listener and didn't press too hard with a lot of questions. Mama knew her child had been hurt, deeply hurt, and it was best not to say too much.

That night as Jodie lay down on her little bed, she watched the starry sky for a long time. She didn't say a goodnight prayer like she usually did. Somehow it just didn't seem right to be thanking God for this and that when she didn't feel very thankful for anything. And she still felt guilty for having been so mad at God and everyone else. Most of the anger was still there, and she knew it might be a very long time before she got rid of it, if she ever did.

The one thing she knew would stick with her forever was her promise never to play baseball again. No, she would never, ever play baseball again.

chapter six

The warm days of June slowly turned into sweltering hot days of July. One day ran into the next, each one exactly like the other, the same routine, day after day. Help Mama with the laundry, make the beds, help Mama clean houses, wash the dishes, baby-sit for Mrs. Turner, and so on and so on. It all added up to the same thing for Jodie—boredom.

Even Saturdays weren't much better. Jodie usually went to Frannie's, and she honestly tried to enjoy the things Frannie liked to do. They played with paper dolls, cut pictures out of magazines, read books out loud to each other, things like that. Frannie was in heaven, but Jodie was bored to death.

But no matter how boring life had become, Jodie stuck to her promise. No baseball. She didn't watch it or talk about it or even think about it. It was still too painful. She hoped the new little league team was losing every game, but she didn't dare bring up the subject to anyone. Besides, she wasn't speaking to boys ever again.

It was on a quick trip to the corner grocery store to get Mama some flour and milk that Jodie found out what she hoped to learn.

The Greenwood Gators were losers.

Two dads were sitting on the store porch discussing the new team when Jodie slipped by unnoticed.

"Just can't understand why our guys can't get things going," Mr. Thompson said as he shook his head in bewilderment.

"Know what you mean," Mr. Davis agreed. "Four losses out of four is pitiful. A downright shame." And he shook his head, too.

"But don't forget about the one forfeit," Mr. Thompson added. "At least, that goes in the win column for us."

"Hmph," snorted Mr. Davis as he took a sip of his cola. "A bus breaking down doesn't mean you won the game. That bunch of Okolona boys would have beaten the socks off our boys."

And the two dads shook their heads in agreement as they focused on the wood planks of the porch floor, sipping at their bottles of Coke and lamenting the failure of the new little league team.

Jodie couldn't hold back the corners of her mouth that were pushing up to form the biggest grin. She couldn't keep her head from shaking over such a stupid name, Greenwood Gators. And she really couldn't keep from thinking, *Serves you right, you losers.*

For the first time in many weeks Jodie's step was almost perky, and her mood was almost happy.

Mama couldn't help noticing this welcome change in her daughter.

"My. You seem awfully happy today," she commented.

Jodie just shrugged her shoulders. She had sworn not to talk about baseball or the team, so there was nothing to say.

Mama wasn't put off so easily.

"Excited about the Fourth of July picnic?" she probed. "It's always so much fun. I know you love it."

Actually, Jodie had forgotten all about the Fourth of July. But since Mama brought it up, that could be a good reason to be in better spirits. Why not? It was one of Jodie's favorite days of the whole year. So Mama and she talked all through dinner about the big picnic, the fireworks, square dancing in the street, watermelons, sack races, and all the fun things they could expect.

The first rays of the morning sun were bright and intense. As usual, July fourth promised to be the hottest day of the summer, or, at least, it always seemed like it. People came from all over, carrying casseroles, sipping on glasses of iced tea, wiping their brows and necks with sweat-stained handkerchiefs. Jodie didn't mind the heat, and she most certainly welcomed the excitement.

As Mama parked the car, Jodie realized she was genuinely excited, a feeling she had not felt in many weeks. She looked forward to playing a game of kick-the-can with someone other that Frannie and Ralph. She couldn't wait to hear the music and watch the people dance. The fried chicken, watermelon, and chocolate cake: she could already taste them. And the fireworks—oh the fireworks!—were her favorite part.

But no matter how quickly her heart was beating or how much she wanted to race across the field to the town square, she knew she must wait on her mother. Mama had a very curious habit of standing back and watching a crowd before actually moving into it. Jodie never understood why Mama was always so nervous, scanning the faces with fearful eyes, almost as if she expected a horrible monster to be waiting on her.

Jodie pretended to have a rock in her shoe. She stomped, slowly squatted down, and took off the shoe. Mama paid no attention as Jodie rubbed her foot and pretended to look for the rock in the toe of her shoe. Mama was too busy studying the people milling around the picnic grounds. Jodie followed her mother's eyes, wondering what in the world she was looking for.

Then, as if a light bulb had gone off in her brain, Jodie knew the answer. In her mind, she could see the face of the woman who looked so much like her mother. She remembered the cold blue eyes that stared without a trace of a smile. She remembered the story of the lost job and how two sisters never spoke to each other. Of course that was it. Why hadn't she thought of it before? Mama was afraid of her sister. And who wouldn't be? Her aunt was a living, breathing, honest-to-goodness witch if there ever was one.

Jodie found herself searching the crowd, too. She had only seen her aunt one time, in the lady's backyard when Jodie was trespassing. How strange it seemed now! You would think in a small town like Greenwood she would have crossed paths with her aunt before. Maybe it was because Mama and Jodie never went where rich folks were. Maybe Rose Parker was one of those people who never came out of her house. Maybe she had servants who did all the shopping while she stayed behind closed doors with the curtains shut. She probably hated people and picnics and fun stuff.

Jodie put her shoe back on and took Mama's hand. It broke her trance and made her smile. No aunt was going to spoil this day. They were off for some good food and fun. Neither of them thought of the wicked sister again.

It felt good to see so many familiar faces. Mama and Jodie returned waves and hellos as they walked through the crowd. Kids were running everywhere. Mothers were busy arranging food on the tables while men huddled in small groups to exchange jokes and talk about politics. There were families they knew from church and friends from school that Jodie hadn't seen since May. Mrs. Turner was there with her new set of twins, and Mama and Jodie each took one in their arms.

"There's Frannie," Jodie squealed and gently laid the baby back in his carriage. "Mama, can I go play with Frannie?"

"Of course, dear," replied Mama as she cooed and patted the twin in her arms. "Go have fun." She called after Jodie, "Don't forget. It's almost time to eat."

Jodie nodded as she ran to catch Frannie. How could Jodie forget about that? She couldn't wait to dig in. But she wanted to get Frannie first. Together they rounded up some other girls from school for a quick game of tag before getting in line to fill their plates.

Jodie had never seen so much food in her life. Her paper plate almost broke under the weight of all the chicken, potato salad, tomatoes, corn on the cob, and watermelon she piled on it. Frannie and Jodie sat under a big oak and laughed and talked as they stuffed their mouths.

"I need more watermelon," exclaimed Jodie, wiping her mouth and spitting out a seed. They both laughed as the seed bounced off Jodie's fork and landed in Frannie's glass of lemonade. "Be right back."

And she headed for a table loaded down with big slices of the juiciest, red watermelon you ever did see. She could already taste that fresh piece of watermelon, and, because she was thinking of nothing else, she was totally surprised by what happened next.

"Hey, kid," a voice called close behind her. Jodie knew immediately who it was. She stopped dead still. Her heart pounded, and her breathing stopped. Her eyes darted from side to side, looking for someone to rescue her. Everyone was too busy to notice a little girl about to be bashed.

She should've been more careful. She should've kept her eyes open for trouble. But danger had come out of nowhere, and now it was too late; Tommy the Terrible was right behind her.

Or maybe not. If she was startled by his voice, it was nothing compared to the shock she got when she spun around. Was this really Tommy the Terrible? Something was wrong. Jodie blinked in surprise. She had never seen Tommy without the faces of his mean buddies, peering over his shoulder at her. She had never seen him in his green and white-striped little league uniform, and she certainly had never seen this embarrassed look on his face. Something weird had taken over his body, and this new Tommy was almost as scary as the old Tommy.

For a few seconds, Tommy didn't look so terrible anymore. But that was as long as it lasted. In another blink of an eye, the old Tommy was back. He put on a growling face and said, "That was some dirty trick you played on us."

Jodie clenched her teeth, making her jaw hard and tight. She was ready for the attack.

Tommy poked her shoulder with his finger, but she stood firm.

"Yeah, you thought you could pull one over on all of us," he continued, jabbing her again with his pointed finger. "But I guess we showed you, huh?"

Jodie began to tremble, not so much in fear but from the thought of that horrible day. She felt tears welling to the surface of her eyes, but she would not cry in front of Tommy the Terrible. She just couldn't.

Tommy gave a little snort and backed away from Jodie. At this moment there were a lot of things Jodie expected to happen—a good sock on the jaw, a terrific shove to the ground, or even a breath-snatching blow to the stomach—all of these things, and more, could come from Tommy the Terrible. But what did happen was totally unexpected.

"You're a girl," he stated, as if she didn't know. "Girls don't play baseball. Not now. Not ever!" He took a deep breath, looked down at the ground and paused. Jodie waited for another explosion. To her surprise, it didn't come.

"But . . . well, uh . . ." he stammered. "You sure can hit."

He shook his head and looked her squarely in the face. "Yep, too bad you're not a boy 'cause you sure can hit."

He turned to go, stopped, and faced her again, this time pointing his finger at her. "Don't tell anyone I said that," he threatened. "Or you'll be sorry."

Then, as quickly as he had appeared, he was out of sight.

Jodie was stunned. Her mouth was open, and her eyes, which only a second ago were filled with tears, were now wide with surprise. It was not possible that this had really happened. No, not possible at all.

Jodie forgot all about the watermelon. She turned and walked slowly back to Frannie, still trying to digest what had just taken place.

"What's the matter with you?" Frannie asked. "All out of watermelon?"

Jodie didn't answer but sat down, still deep in thought. Tommy the Terrible had actually said something nice to her, at least it seemed like it. He had such a hateful way of spitting words out at her that "you're beautiful" would sound like a death threat. But yes, he had said she could really hit. That made her feel good. But she was also confused and shocked and angry.

"Jo-o-die! What's the matter with you?" Frannie was aggravated because she couldn't get her friend to answer. This shook Jodie back to reality. Tommy's last words, the threat, were still ringing in her ears.

53

"Oh, nothing," was all Jodie said.

So Jodie tried to chit-chat with Frannie just to keep her friend happy. Jodie talked about the food and the people and why all these stupid boys were wearing their baseball uniforms. In every direction Jodie could see boys running around in green and white stripes.

"They think they're hot stuff in those uniforms," Jodie said because she was so jealous about not having one herself. "I bet they're burning up in them. It'd serve them right if they had a heat stroke. They just want everybody to look at them and . . . "

"They're not showing off," Frannie interrupted Jodie to shut her up. "They're playing a game today. They have to wear them."

This stung Jodie like an angry hornet. It hadn't occurred to her that the team could be playing a game today. Not today. Not here. Not on her day to have fun.

"Didn't you know that?" Frannie asked with surprise. "Everybody's been talking about it for days. Everybody will get to see the new little league team play."

"Yeah. You mean watch them *lose*," Jodie snapped at Frannie, startling her and making her big-rimmed glasses drop to the end of her nose. Jodie's face was hot with anger. They had no right to play baseball in front of her at *her* Fourth of July picnic.

"Well, don't get mad at *me*," Frannie snapped back. "Nobody says you have to watch it."

"You're right about that," Jodie agreed, standing up and slapping the grass off the back of her shorts. "And I don't intend to watch now or *ever*. I'm going home!"

Jodie stomped away to find her mother. Frannie called after her, but it did no good. Jodie wouldn't stay there for all the money in the city bank. She would not stick around to see all those goofy boys prance around in their goofy uniforms. She would not listen to the crowd cheer for boys who couldn't hit a baseball if it were the size of a pumpkin. She did not want to see baseball, hear about baseball, or think about baseball. And it just wasn't right to spoil her day with it.

Jodie pushed through crowds of people. Where was her mother anyway? She stomped around the picnic grounds until she saw a small group of women clustered under a large oak tree. There was Mama sitting in a borrowed lawn chair, fanning herself, and laughing softly. Jodie sneaked around the tree and came up behind Mama. She didn't want the other ladies to stare and make a fuss with "oh how you've grown" and all that stuff women say to little kids.

"Mama," whispered Jodie.

"Oh, hon', what are you doing here?" Mama was startled by the voice behind her. "I thought you'd be playing with Frannie and the other kids. Did you get something to eat?"

"Yes, Mama, I got plenty," she answered calmly. "Can I go home?"

Mama shot up from her lawn chair.

"Are you sick? Did you stuff yourself with cake?" Mama began to pound Jodie with questions in that frantic way only mothers can when they're worried about their children. "You didn't eat a whole watermelon, did you? Or those peppers, the little red ones that burn your mouth so? Let me feel your head. Maybe you've been run . . . "

"No, Mama," Jodie insisted, pushing her mother's hand away. "I'm not sick. I just want to go home."

This seemed to worry Mama more than a tummy-ache. She knew what to do about that kind of problem. But these new problems, the hurt feelings and disappointment, were a whole lot more complicated. Mama could tell when her daughter was hurt, but she was helpless in fixing it and didn't know what to do. Mama knew something had happened to spoil her child's good day.

"Okay, hon'," she said. "Let's go."

"No, Mama," Jodie put her hand on Mama's arm. "You stay and have a good time. I can walk. It's not far at all."

"Heavens no, child," Mama protested. She smoothed her dress, coughed, then took a deep breath. "Besides, I'm getting a little tired myself. I've had enough fun for one day."

So mother and daughter walked together to the car and spent the rest of the afternoon quietly at home. Mama took a very long nap while Jodie moped around, doing anything that would take her mind off the picnic, her friends, and baseball. She tried moving the furniture in her tiny bedroom but gave up when she decided it could only fit one way, the way it was to begin with. Going outside to catch beetles, she came across only one grasshopper, three spiders, and a wasp's nest, none of which she cared to mess with. She even tried playing a game of tag by herself but soon tired out from running around the yard with nobody after her.

The longest day soon turned into night. Mama and Jodie sat on the porch and watched the fireflies blinking around the yard like so many stars in the sky. It was peaceful and warm, and the air had that good summer smell. They both sat quietly, deep in thought.

"Mama," Jodie finally broke the silence. "How long will you take roses to Daddy's grave?"

If the question surprised Mama she did not show it. Her breathing was steady, and she didn't move a muscle. In a few minutes she answered, "I guess as long as I live."

They both sat silently again, each thinking about the answer.

"You see, Jodie," Mama spoke up. "When you love someone, love him or her more than anything else in the world, it never goes away." Mama reached over and took Jodie's hand. Jodie scooted close to her mother and put her head in Mama's lap. Mama combed Jodie's hair with her fingers. "Even if that person dies, the love never dies. It's always in your heart, and you never forget."

Jodie lay still and listened. She liked the sound of her mother's voice. She liked to hear her mother talk about feelings. She liked the feel of her mother's fingers in her hair.

"It's like the way I love you," Mama continued. "It only grows deeper every day. Love just grows and grows until you love someone more than your very own life. That's the way I love you, and that's the way I love your daddy." Mama seemed to be drifting into that world of her own that she rarely shared with Jodie. "One day when you're older, you'll understand."

There she goes again, Jodie thought. *Always saying when I'm older.*

Jodie wanted to understand now.

Then Mama added, "I'll love you and your daddy till my last breath. So, sweetheart, I guess there'll be a rose on that grave until then."

Just then a loud explosion jarred Jodie and Mama out of their dreamlike thoughts. The sky lit up in bright, dazzling sparkles.

"Fireworks!" Jodie squealed and jumped up from her mother's lap. Another blast of blue and red lights quickly followed the first. "Look, Mama! It's the fireworks!"

"I didn't know you could see them so good from here," her mother exclaimed. "They're beautiful!"

As quickly as one colorful burst died away, another rose to take its place. Jodie and Mama *oohed* and *aahed* with each bang and flash of sparkling light. The sky filled with tiny bright stars of all different colors. Jodie was thrilled. She loved the fireworks. It was her favorite part of the whole Fourth of July day. And she had the best seat, right there on her own porch beside her mother. All the disappointments of the day and of the summer melted away, and she was filled with happiness and love.

She thought of what Mrs. McGuffy, who was about a hundred years old and lived next to them in their other house, once said to her, "The good Lord should give us a way to bottle up a really good feeling, for later, when we need it." Jodie wished she could. Then, if things got bad, she could just open that bottled up good feeling. She wanted to be this warm and happy always.

If Jodie could have magically seen into the future as she sat on the porch that night, she would know her happiness would not last. Things would get bad, very bad. And she would also discover that she had bottled up the good feeling. It would always be in her heart and in her memories.

chapter seven

Jodie looked around the room at all the solemn faces. It was the first day of school, and all the students acted as if they had been sentenced to life in prison. They were frozen in position, afraid to move, as they listened to the high, piercing voice of Mrs. Rutherford, the fourth grade teacher. According to the Presbyterian kids, she often sang solos at church, and, whenever she did, babies cried, adults winced, and little kids plugged their ears with their fingers.

All eyes followed Mrs. Rutherford as she waddled back and forth in front of the desks. No one moved a muscle or dared breathe too loudly. But it soon became obvious that everyone was hearing the same annoying sound. *Swish, swish, swish.* With each step—*swish.* Eyes darted from side to side. Eyebrows wrinkled in puzzlement. What *was* that sound? When Jodie finally realized it was Mrs. Rutherford's large legs in nylon stockings rubbing together, she had to cover her mouth to hide her giggle. Jodie wanted to look back at Frannie, who was sitting two desks back, but she didn't dare. She knew then that fourth grade would be hard. Hard on the brains, hard on the ears, and even harder to keep a straight face.

Jodie wasn't too wild about school in the first place. But she had to admit it was good to be back with kids her age and away from the many chores at home. It had been a long, hard summer for Mama and for her. But things would be better soon. The many fields of cotton would have to be picked, and Mama could get better work at the gin. Jodie worried more and more about her mother, and she would be glad when Mama didn't have to do so much laundry and house-cleaning. Mama was sick, and although it was not something Jodie and Mama could talk about, they both knew it. Jodie felt helpless, and all she could do about it was help Mama as much as possible. That meant coming straight home from school every day and working till supper time.

Suddenly, a large, wooden ruler came down in front of Jodie's face and landed on her desk. Mrs. Rutherford was standing over Jodie and peering down at her over the thin rim of her glasses. Jodie had been daydreaming again. This was a problem for her in third grade, and she knew that all bad things about kids were always passed along to the next teacher. Mrs. Rutherford already had her eye on Jodie.

". . . to learn to listen," the teacher was saying, still peering down at Jodie. "It is most important in fourth grade. You must pay close attention at all times. This is a responsibility of a fourth grader."

Jodie looked up at Mrs. Rutherford with her best listening face, and she really tried hard to keep her mind on her new teacher's words of wisdom. But the close-up sight of Mrs. Rutherford's hippo-like hips started Jodie wondering how in the world she had gotten down the row of desks without knocking everybody and everything out of the way. As if the teacher could read Jodie's thoughts, Mrs. Rutherford tugged at her dress and smoothed the waist. Then she backed down the narrow space between the desks as students leaned over sideways holding onto their books and papers to keep from being swept away with the rolling tide. Jodie nearly choked on the giggle that rose in her throat.

Yes, there was no doubt. This would be a hard year, a very hard year.

And as the day wore on, things didn't get any better. When it was finally recess, Jodie was exhausted. Just thinking about the spelling tests and flipping through the new textbooks was enough to wear her out. But at least recess would not be a problem for Jodie this year. She had started the first day of fourth grade

feeling good about that. For one thing, she would not be trying to break into the boys' games. This would keep Tommy the Terrible, who was in fifth grade, and his friends off her back. Besides, ever since the Fourth of July picnic she wasn't all that terrified of him anymore. She was pretty sure he would stay clear of her.

Jodie and Frannie joined a small group of girls sitting under a tree. They spent much of the time talking about Mrs. Rutherford and laughing till their sides hurt. She had been the fourth grade teacher for about a hundred years, or at least it seemed like it. Mothers, fathers, aunts, and uncles of Greenwood had all been taught by Mrs. Rutherford. Everyone knew about her famous two-inch wooden paddle. It was no secret how red her face could get or how shrill her voice became whenever a student angered her.

At first, Jodie was laughing as the other girls told stories about older brothers and sisters who had experienced Mrs. Rutherford's fourth grade. But then she stopped laughing. A curtain of silence dropped over her, and a worried look spread across her face. She had the strangest feeling she would meet that famous two-inch paddle. Sensing that she would know the wrath of her infamous teacher, Jodie was not sure if she would survive fourth grade at all.

That night, as she helped Mama fold clothes, she chattered away about everything that had happened at school. Mama couldn't keep from laughing when Jodie imitated Mrs. Rutherford, swishing her hips back and forth across the kitchen. It made Mama smile when Jodie talked about the games she played with the girls and how much fun it had been. Mama was happy that all the fuss about baseball was gone.

What Jodie didn't tell Mama about was all the fear she had about fourth grade. She didn't tell Mama about the paddle or Mrs. Rutherford's ruler coming down on her desk, already on the first day. She didn't tell Mama about the hard work or the thirty spelling words she had to learn each week. Some things were better kept to herself. What Mama didn't know wouldn't worry her. Jodie would worry enough for both of them.

As one school day rolled into another, Jodie could not escape the watchful eye of Mrs. Rutherford. Her large shadow loomed over Jodie's desk from early morning till the dismissal bell. The teacher seemed to pinpoint the exact minute Jodie fell into daydreaming and would snap her out of it by asking a question Jodie had not heard and could not answer. Jodie felt like a tiny mouse being stalked by a very large cat, and, any day, the cat's strong paw would come crashing down to crush Jodie.

And it did. At least, Jodie thought so. It happened the last day of September, a beautiful, cool afternoon, the kind of day that makes you antsy all day for the dismissal bell to ring. Just when it did, Jodie grabbed her sweater and was ready to bolt out the door with Frannie when she heard the dreaded words.

"Jodie Mills," Mrs. Rutherford said, never looking up from the papers she was grading. "Stay put a few minutes. I need to speak to you."

Jodie and Frannie stopped dead in their tracks. Here it was. The dreaded paw was coming down. Jodie looked at Frannie for help. Frannie returned a look full of terror and scooted quickly out the door. Jodie glanced around the room. Everybody was gone, leaving her alone with Mrs. Rutherford. Gulping and turning to face Mrs. Rutherford's desk, Jodie clutched her notebook and books close to her chest and waited.

Mrs. Rutherford seemed to have forgotten Jodie was there as the teacher continued peering over the papers in front of her, marking a check here and a circle there with her red pen. Jodie's leg was cramping, but she was afraid to move. She needed a drink of water, but she didn't dare clear her throat. Her fears were mounting with each second, and it seemed like an eternity before Mrs. Rutherford finally stabbed her red pen into her graying French roll. She always kept her pens and pencils in her bundled-up hair, sometimes having as many as three or four of them at one time. Then she looked like some kind of weird bug or space alien with little antennae sticking up, something else her students laughed about at recess. Right then, she had two pens in place, but Jodie wasn't giggling.

Mrs. Rutherford stared at Jodie over the rim of her glasses, a look Jodie had seen far too many times in the last few weeks. Then the teacher took off her glasses and looked at Jodie again. Jodie was surprised to see, looking at her teacher now in this way, that the woman had very pretty blue eyes. Eyes that were soft and warm. Eyes that were looking at Jodie in a very unusual way as if Mrs. Rutherford was looking for something on the girl's face.

Jodie held her breath and waited for her teacher to speak.

"How's your mother, dear?" Mrs. Rutherford said softly. Her voice didn't sound so high-pitched and shrill now.

Surprised by the question, Jodie couldn't get any words out. She had expected a scolding at best, but not this.

"She gets a little tired," Jodie said so softly that Mrs. Rutherford had to lean over her big desk to hear. Jodie cleared her dry throat and tried again.

"She's tired all the time," Jodie said much louder. "She sleeps a lot. And she coughs a lot. But she says she's fine."

Mrs. Rutherford nodded and leaned back in her chair. She kept looking at Jodie with her gentle eyes.

"You know, Jodie," she said. "I was once your mother's teacher. She sat in that front desk, right over there." Mrs. Rutherford pointed with an old, crooked finger to a desk behind Jodie. Jodie turned to look at it. She could not imagine her mother as a little girl who had once sat in that small desk. But she could tell Mrs. Rutherford was remembering as if it were yesterday.

"Daisy was a good student," she continued. "Sweetest girl. Yes, she was a joy."

Oh, dear, thought Jodie. *Here it comes. A why-can't-you-be-more-like-your-mother speech.*

Mrs. Rutherford leaned forward and folded her hands on her desk. Jodie swallowed hard. Her throat was so dry she thought she might choke. Her hands were getting sweaty from gripping her books so tightly. But she stood patiently and waited for the sermon.

"I knew your daddy, too," Mrs. Rutherford said. Jodie was so surprised she wasn't sure if she had heard correctly. "He was a fine young man. As fine as they come."

Now Mrs. Rutherford was not looking at Jodie. The teacher was looking past Jodie like Mama did when she drifted into that world of her own. Mrs. Rutherford seemed to be talking to herself, remembering out loud like some people do when they think about the past. She talked on about Jodie's mother and father as if Jodie were not in the room.

"It was a sad day when your daddy went off to war," remembered Mrs. Rutherford. She paused, and Jodie could see her eyes fill with tears. "It was the saddest day when they brought him home." She pulled a tissue from the box on her desk and dabbed her eyes. Then she returned her glasses back to their place on the tip of her nose, and the old Mrs. Rutherford was back. Jodie felt like she had been dreaming the last few minutes as she waited for her teacher to get down to business with her.

Mrs. Rutherford stared at Jodie again. The soft eyes looked harsh now as she peered over her glasses. But the scolding never came.

"You know, dear," she continued in a soft voice. "You look like your daddy." She nodded as if agreeing with herself. "Yes, a lot like your daddy."

Then to dismiss Jodie she added, "Please tell your mother hello for me. I'll try to get by to see her real soon."

Jodie was afraid to move. There had been no sharp words, no warnings, no red face, no rulers or two-inch paddles. She couldn't believe it was over.

"Go on, now. I've kept you long enough." Mrs. Rutherford waved her hand, watching Jodie over the top of her glasses. She gave Jodie a little smile, and, to Jodie's surprise, she found herself smiling back.

As she walked down the steps of the old schoolhouse, she couldn't help thinking that old Mrs. Hippo-hips wasn't too bad after all. Jodie felt like she was walking out of a dream, and she was thinking about it so hard that she didn't see the bushes shake as she walked past. She didn't see the body jump out or the hands grab her shoulders.

Jodie screamed and dropped her books. She spun around and was face to face with worried little Frannie, who was studying Jodie's face for tear stains, checking her body for bruises or broken bones.

"What happened?" Frannie asked frantically.

Jodie caught her breath and sputtered, "*You* is what happened. You scared me to death!"

Together they picked up Jodie's things and walked toward the road.

"Well, did she get all red in the face?" Frannie persisted. "Did she scream real loud?"

"Nope," was all Jodie would say.

"What was she mad about?" Frannie kept on. "She heard you making fun of her at lunch, didn't she? *That* was it. I *knew* it."

Jodie just shook her head and kept walking. It was fun making her excited little friend wait to hear the truth. Besides, Jodie was still trying to sort things out herself. It had been a very unexpected visit with the teacher she had feared so much, and she didn't know what to make of it.

"*Jo-o-o-die,*" whined Frannie, as she stopped in the road to stomp her foot. Jodie knew Frannie was dying from the suspense, and she had been patient long enough.

"Okay, okay," grinned Jodie. "She wanted to know how Mama was feeling."

Frannie looked at Jodie in disbelief.

"That was it?"

"That was it," answered Jodie still smiling. "No screaming, no paddling, no red face. Just wanted to talk about my mama. . . and . . . and my daddy."

Frannie's mouth dropped open. Then she shut it quickly. Jodie never talked about her daddy, and Frannie knew it was not a subject she ever wanted to bring up. They continued their walk home, neither friend saying a word, both thinking about the strange after-school meeting.

Then Frannie spoke up, "Not even a little bawling out?"

Jodie grinned wide and started to giggle. This made Frannie's puzzled face soften, and in a few seconds she was giggling, too. Neither girl knew why, but when you feel good from the inside out, giggling is what happens.

Just then a loud farm truck pulled onto the road behind the two girls. Jodie and Frannie jumped into the shallow ditch that ran alongside the road as the truck bounced and grinded past them. A large cloud of dust covered them, and they coughed and rubbed their eyes. Through the haze they could see heads and hats sticking up from the tall sideboards of the truck bed. Jodie let out a whoop and jumped back onto the dusty road.

"They're here!" she cried. "Hot dog! It's time to pick cotton!"

Frannie and Jodie ran down the road, out of sheer joy, after the truck which was already out of sight. The truck had been loaded down with workers from Mexico. They were headed to the many small houses on cotton farms all around the area. This truck meant only one thing to Jodie. The cotton was ready to be picked, and soon the gins would be running full blast. And that meant Mama would have a better job and be making more money. Then she would get well. Jodie was sure of it.

The two girls ran and laughed all the way to Jodie's yard where they fell out on the soft green grass and lay there catching their breath. Jodie watched the clouds and the clear blue sky and started thinking. *Some days are just bad, bad from daylight to nighttime, everything that happens to you is just bad. But some days are chock full of good things, one surprise after another, and you never know when either kind of day is going to happen.* Today was one of those good days. It had just come out of nowhere, but here it was, a super happy *good* day. She loved the warm feeling she felt inside. All her worries about fourth grade and Mrs. Rutherford disappeared. All her worries about Mama and the hard work and money seemed small now. Everything was going to be fine.

chapter eight

Just as Jodie had expected, Mama started work at the gin the following Monday. That Monday after school, instead of going home, Jodie walked to the gin to see Mama. She was very busy, punching numbers into a small adding machine and writing something in a big book. Jodie liked to sit by her mother's desk and watch the little machine print out numbers on the narrow white paper that got longer and longer till it streamed down to the floor. It looked like fun to Jodie. Mama always gave her the discarded rolls of paper whenever she replaced them with new, bigger ones, and Jodie would write stories or draw pictures on them while she waited for Mama to go home.

What Jodie liked best was to walk around the gin, watching the large trailers of cotton being pulled under the huge, sucking tubes. When things got really busy there was usually a long line of trailers all loaded to the top with fluffy, white cotton. Only two trailers could be emptied at a time. Men would climb into the trailers and vacuum up the soft white stuff with a big metal cylinder. This looked like even more fun than punching numbers on the adding machine.

While Jodie was watching all this hustle and bustle, a nice man who worked inside the gin motioned her to come over. The machines were so loud he had to shout.

"Want to have a look around?"

Jodie nodded and stepped inside. The noise was even louder, and Jodie had to put her fingers in her ears. But she couldn't believe her eyes! The machines were as high as the two-story building she had entered, and cotton was falling like gigantic, fluffy waterfalls on the belts of each machine. Jodie watched in amazement. Then she followed the little white balls of cotton as they danced on the conveyor belts. Somehow these noisy machines were shaking out all the dirt and leaves and removing the seeds before the cotton could be baled. Jodie was fascinated.

She would have stayed there for hours, but her new friend motioned her to walk to the end of the room. There the clean cotton was being pressed into huge bales, wrapped in burlap cloth, and bound with long metal strips. Then she watched more men put the heavy bales on iron racks with rollers and push them to the loading dock. Even in the first day of October the workers were sweaty from the hard work. Jodie decided that this was one job that didn't look like any fun at all.

When Jodie followed the man outside, away from the noisy machines, her ears were still ringing. She learned that his name was Roscoe, Mr. Roscoe, she would call him. Jodie introduced herself and explained that she was waiting on her mother who worked in the gin office.

"Well, that's just fine," Mr. Roscoe said. "You come back tomorrow and watch this ol' gin get fired up again. It sure can move some cotton along."

Jodie thanked him and knew she would be back. She would bring Frannie, and the two of them would have a ball exploring around the gin. It was a good plan, but it never happened.

The days were getting shorter, and Mama's working days were getting longer. When the cotton was coming in this quickly, everyone worked into the night, so after that first day, Jodie could no longer play around the gin until Mama got off. Jodie would stop by to see Mama, do a little homework beside her mother's desk, then she would have to walk home before it got dark. There was supper to get on the table, and chores to be done. Even before the first week was over, Mama's old car pulled in the driveway later and later each night. Mama would be so tired, she would take only a few bites of supper and head straight to bed.

By Sunday morning Jodie decided the job at the gin might not be the answer to her mother's illness. She did not remember Mama being so tired when she worked there last fall, even with the long hours. So when Jodie heard her mother shuffling down the hall, coughing and heaving as if each breath were her last, Jodie had to speak up.

"Mama, go back to bed," Jodie pleaded. "We can miss church one time. There's no harm in that."

Mama shook her head as she coughed again.

"No, I'm okay," she protested. "Just takes me a little longer to get my engine going, that's all."

Jodie knew not to argue. It would only cause her mother to cough more and use good breath that didn't need to be wasted on an argument. The best thing to do was help Mama all Jodie could by getting breakfast and being in the car when it was time to go.

As Mama tried to start the old car Jodie couldn't tell which one sounded worse—Mama with her coughing and wheezing or the rattletrap that sputtered, popped, and rumbled with each twist of the key.

"This ol' piece of junk," grumbled Jodie. "One of these days it's just gonna give a groan and die." And as soon as Jodie had said this, she wished she hadn't. At least they had a car, even if it was as old as she was, and she knew Mama would want to remind her of this blessing in a nice long speech.

But it was more than that. Jodie gave a shudder just thinking about the car dying, never to start up again. She was afraid to look at Mama, so she stared out the car window as they pulled away. Mama didn't say a word about the car or Jodie's comment. She probably hadn't heard it. It was like Mama to be deep in thought on the drive to church, probably because of the roses on the back seat.

Jodie didn't have to peek over the seat to see if they were there. She knew they were. Not one Sunday had gone by without them. She had stopped wondering about the secret rose. It did no good to ask or try to talk about it. She decided she would never know, that it would always be her mother's secret.

But that changed today.

70

Mama pulled the car over to the curb, but instead of getting out herself, she turned to Jodie.

"Jodie, dear," she almost whispered. "I'm especially tired this morning." She coughed a terrible deep cough, laying her delicate hand on her chest as if in pain. "I don't think I can make the walk."

Jodie waited silently for her mother to get out the next words. She expected her to suggest that they go back home which was just fine with Jodie. She knew Mama needed to go back to bed. But she wasn't ready for what she heard.

"Please, dear, would you take the rose for me today?"

Jodie was shocked. Her wide eyes looked at Mama in disbelief. She couldn't be serious. But when Mama turned to look at Jodie, she never looked so serious in her life.

"Now, listen carefully, please," Mama began her instructions. "You know to go down and around the corner." Jodie nodded her head. This much she knew, having watched her mother so many times.

"Walk down the sidewalk. You'll be walking beside a tall, white wooden fence. Then you'll pass an alley." Mama burst into another fit of coughing. Jodie waited patiently, trying to remember everything she was hearing. Mama finally caught her breath.

"When you pass the alley, you'll see a row of very tall bushes."

Jodie nodded her head, thinking about what the bushes might look like.

"There's a small path through the bushes. Look carefully and you'll see where the grass hasn't grown for years. Slip through this opening in the bushes, and when you do, you'll see a white house. It's only a few steps to the side porch. Leave the rose on the top step and come right back. There's no time to dawdle," Mama finished with a smile.

"But, Mama, what if . . . "

"It'll be all right," Mama assured her. "I promise. Just leave the rose on the top step and scoot on back here."

71

"But, Mama, who lives . . . "

"Now hurry or we'll be late for church," Mama was not answering any questions.

Jodie sighed and obeyed her mother. She stretched over the front seat and picked up one of the roses. Then she jerked on the door handle, gave the old door a hard shove with her shoulder, and headed off on her mission.

Around the corner and along the white fence she walked, biting her lip and feeling edgy about her task. Now that her mother and car were out of sight, she was scared. She knew her mother made this same walk every Sunday, but that was Mama. She was a grown-up. Jodie was a different story. She was just a little girl, and something was going to get her. Her heart began to beat faster as she approached the alley. Everything was very quiet, too quiet.

Jodie saw the row of bushes. They were tall, so tall they hid the house that was behind them. All she could see was the roof and second floor windows of a very large, white house. She had stopped and was looking up at the sight when a car drove by and startled her. This got her moving again as she searched the ground for the secret path.

There it was, a trodden-down dirt path that was easy to see, but not easy to get through. The bushes scratched Jodie's face as she plunged into them. She fought the leaves and branches, and for a few seconds she thought she might suffocate until she suddenly broke through to fresh air. She found herself in a yard covered with yellow and brown fall leaves. Just as Mama had said, there was a porch, a side door to the big white house, and a large window with a white lace curtain beside the door. Jodie knew to take a few steps and place the rose on the top step, but her feet wouldn't move. There was something very creepy about this place. Something a lot creepier about leaving the rose. It was like leaving the other rose at the cold headstone at her daddy's grave. This was a cold house. Was there a dead person inside?

Jodie knew she had to help Mama, so she took a deep breath and stepped forward. Nothing happened. Jodie looked around, checking behind her for good measure. She took another step. Nothing stirred. In the next two steps, she was at the porch. Stretching as far as she could without moving her body any closer, she dropped the delicate rose on the step. At that moment the little hairs on the back of her neck began to tingle. She felt goose bumps on her arms. She could feel eyes on her. Somebody was watching her; she just knew it.

Jodie jumped back and looked around again. There was no one in sight. She caught her breath and stood perfectly still. The only sound was the singing of a bird on the roof. She took a step backwards without turning her back on the house; she was sure someone had been watching her. Then, feeling a little silly, Jodie took another deep breath and headed back to the bushes.

There it was. Just as she turned to go, out of the corner of her eye, she saw it. The curtain moved. She was sure she saw fingertips at the bottom edge of the lace. But she was not looking twice. Jodie scurried like a little squirrel back through the wall of the bushes and hit the sidewalk running. She ran as fast as she could, which was very hard to do in black patent Sunday shoes, past the alley and beside the white wooden fence. A dog growled and barked at her from the other side, running along as if trying to bite her through the fence. This made her run even faster, and her heart was beating as fast as her feet were running.

But she didn't dare let Mama see her in such a state. At the corner, Jodie put on the brakes, skidding and sliding in her slick-bottom shoes. She ran her fingers through her matted hair, picking out a few leaves, straightened her hair bow, tugged at her dress, and pulled her sweater together in the front. Stepping around the corner as cool and calm as she could pretend to be, she strolled slowly to the car, smiling at Mama to let her know everything had gone okay.

When Jodie slid onto the car seat, Mama quickly pulled away from the curb. Jodie was glad Mama didn't ask any questions because she was still out of breath and couldn't talk. Mama simply reached over and patted her on the leg and said, "Thanks, hon'."

The morning's experience had started Jodie to thinking. While Brother Stevens was preaching, she was thinking: thinking about the white house, the rose, and the lace curtain. At least, it was no longer a secret what Mama did with the second rose every Sunday. But there were so many questions still unanswered. And all she could do was think about it.

After church on the way to the cemetery, Jodie was still thinking. She thought while she sat in the car and watched her mother carry the remaining rose to her husband's grave. Jodie closed her eyes and tried to see the white fence and the alley and the big white house. She didn't think she had ever seen the house before. She didn't think she had ever been in that part of town before, but something was very familiar to her. *Who lived in the house? Why did Mama leave a rose there? What could it all mean?* She didn't have a clue.

Then, because she had been thinking about it so hard and for so long, it finally came to her. She *had* been in that part of town before. She remembered the alley. In her mind she could see the back gates that opened into the big backyards of the rich people. She remembered a terrifying day when she went into one of those backyards. Was it the same white house? It was hard to say because she had been so scared and so awed by the beautiful roses in the yard that she had not noticed the details of the house.

But that couldn't be. Mama would never take a rose to a mean woman like Rose Parker, even if they were sisters. They didn't even speak. They hated each other. None of this made any sense to Jodie. No, it couldn't be the same house.

But on the following Sunday, Jodie knew that it was. Again Mama was too weak to take the rose herself, and again Jodie made the journey for her. This time she looked closely at everything around her. Yes, it was the same alley. Jeff's house was down that way somewhere. And yes, it looked like the same fence around the yard in which she had trespassed.

As Jodie pushed through the bushes for the second time, it occurred to her that she was trespassing again. There was every reason to be scared now that she knew who lived in the house. She didn't take her eyes off the curtain in the window beside the porch as she headed toward it. The white lace hung still and lifeless.

Just as she was reaching out to lay the precious rose on the step, the curtain flew back. Jodie was so startled she stumbled backwards. Her shoes slipped on the dewy leaves that covered the ground, and she fell down flat on her back. In a frenzy to get away, her legs pumped and her heels dug into the soft lawn, like a car spinning its tires in the mud. She was getting nowhere fast.

Finally she struggled back to her feet. As she raced for the bushes, she glanced back at the window and saw clearly the thing that had scared her to death. It was a cat. A gray and white cat had jumped up on the window sill and was calmly licking its paw, probably wondering about the silly girl who was lying on the ground. If Jodie felt a little foolish, it didn't matter now. All she wanted was the safety of her car and her mother.

Jodie pushed the incident out of her mind. It was a cat; that was all. And because all the kids at school were buzzing about Halloween just around the corner, costumes and candy and soaping windows, it was easy not to think about the weird event that happened on Sunday. Until one afternoon when all Mrs. Rutherford's fourth graders were reading a story about an Indian boy paddling his canoe and looking for a sacred eagle, Jodie's mind drifted to the cat in the window. She could see its pretty white paws and patches of gray. She thought how nice it would be to pet and hold the cat; she had always wanted one.

As she daydreamed it came to her that there was something else in the picture. She had seen something else that morning. Closing her eyes tightly, she tried hard to see the window again. Yes, it was something blue. For a split second, as the cat pulled back the curtain, something, or rather *someone*, was there. A chill ran through her. Again, someone had been watching her.

"And what do you think happened to the eagle?" Mrs. Rutherford's voice broke Jodie's thoughts. "Uh. . .Jodie Mills. Can you answer that for us?"

Jodie was caught again. She slowly slid down in her seat and began searching the page of her book in a frantic effort to find the answer. All eyes were on her, and it just about burned a hole through her. She glanced around and realized she was not even on the same page as everyone else.

"I don't know," Jodie confessed. There were a few snickers.

Mrs. Rutherford shook her head in that what-am-I-going-to-do-with-you look and moved on to another student. Red-faced, Jodie slowly turned the page to get back in step with the story. She was relieved, at least, that Mrs. Rutherford had not scolded her in front of everybody.

After school that day all the kids hung around outside to talk about their Halloween costumes. Most of the boys were going to be vampires or pirates. The girls chose witches, princesses, and gypsies. The excitement became electric as the big day drew closer, and it was hard to think about anything else.

As Jodie and Frannie walked home together, Frannie chattered away about the red hoopskirt she was borrowing from her big sister and the shiny gold clip-on earrings her Aunt Bess was letting her wear and her mother's old high-heeled shoes. But Jodie kept quiet. She didn't have a costume and had no idea what to do. Mama had been working so late at night and was so tired when she got home that Jodie didn't dare ask her to make one. Jodie was running out of time, but that didn't stop her from getting excited about Halloween. It was one of the most fun days of the whole year. She could hardly wait.

She was so excited that she laid her books down in the road, pulled her sweater over her head, *oo-oo-oohed* like a ghost, and chased Frannie around in circles. They both squealed and laughed. They loved the scary things that came with Halloween.

Just then, a huge, dark cloud blocked the sun, casting a black shadow over the girls. A sudden, cold wind whirled the dust and leaves around them. It sent a shiver through Jodie's whole body, not so much from the cold but from a strange, ominous feeling that stopped her dead still. The feeling was so strong that Jodie became frightened, not of masks and costumes and pretend ghosts, but of real-life kinds of bad things. It was a feeling that something bad was going to happen, and it did not leave her as she ran down the road to find her mother.

chapter nine

Poor Mrs. Rutherford! Pale as a ghost with her hair sticking out in all directions, she slumped behind her desk. The teacher looked like she had just wrestled ten wild polecats, which may have been an easier job than trying to teach lessons and keep order in a classroom on Halloween day. Since first thing that morning, the room mothers had been bouncing in with trays of cupcakes, apples for bobbing, goody bags, and a real jack-o-lantern. Even Mrs. Rutherford's shrill voice, evil eye, and waving ruler could not keep her fourth graders' attention away from all this excitement. She had survived the party and the school day and was now overcome with exhaustion as she watched the noisy herd of children clamber out.

Her students, on the other hand, were just getting started. Everyone raced for the big double-doors, pushing and dropping papers as they stepped on each other in their efforts to get out. Frannie and Jodie knew exactly where they were headed.

"Hey, Pete!" Jodie and Frannie said at the same time as they entered the drug store. They went to Pete's store first because they knew they could count on a free piece of candy to get Halloween started off right.

"Hey, girls," Pete smiled. He slowly wiped the counter and pretended to forget that today was Halloween. "What can I do for you?"

Jodie and Frannie looked at each other in a puzzled way, then back at Pete who just kept wiping the counter.

Finally Jodie spoke up. "Well, trick or treat."

"Trick or treat?" Pete asked, still teasing them. "Well, I'll be a monkey's uncle. It *is* Halloween, isn't it?"

Both girls laughed, and their eyes lit up when Pete brought out a big basket full of candy, not just the penny-kind, but chocolate bars and jawbreakers and stuff. They studied their choices carefully before gently picking up one.

"Thanks, Pete!" both girls exclaimed. They wiggled with excitement on their stools.

Pete put his elbow on the counter and looked at each girl squarely in the face. He sounded very serious when he said, "Now you know, this candy is my insurance that there'll be no window soaping here tonight."

Jodie and Frannie both knew he was still teasing. Pete didn't really mind if you soaped his window; it took only some scrubbing to get the soap-writing off the windows. He just didn't like the mean stuff like throwing raw eggs at his store, breaking things, or spray painting on his sidewalk. That's why he gave candy to kids before he closed up and went home. Nobody would hurt Pete's store. He was nice to kids, and everybody liked him.

"No sir, Pete," Jodie answered. "Promise."

Frannie didn't answer because she had already stuffed a piece of taffy in her mouth, which made her teeth stick together. All she could do was grunt and nod. At the exact same time, both girls made the sign of an *x* over their heart with two fingers, then held the fingers up in a sort of salute. This made Pete lean back and let out a big, hearty laugh.

"Well, Pete," Jodie said. "We gotta go. Mama's waiting for me."

"So long, girls," he chuckled. "Have fun tonight."

Then, as the girls slipped off their stools, he added, "Hey, by the way, what are you girls going to be tonight?"

Frannie smacked, worked her mouth around still trying to unloose the taffy, and managed to mumble, "Gypsy."

Then, because she knew Jodie did not have a costume, Frannie gave her a nervous look. To Frannie's surprise, Jodie beamed and said, "A hobo. I'm going to be a hobo."

Jodie looked at her little friend and smiled. "Thought of it just this morning. Pretty good, huh?"

They turned to leave just as a large group of fifth-grade boys appeared in front of Pete's store. Like a human tornado they pushed through the door bringing noise and confusion with them. Jodie's heart skipped a beat as she heard a dreaded voice, Tommy the Terrible. She grabbed Frannie by the wrist and moved to hide behind a display of magazines, but it was too late.

"Hey y'all," called Nick above the laughing and poking. "Look at the two scary witches." He pointed to Jodie and Frannie. Jodie stared back with her meanest look.

"What ugly masks!" He threw up his hands to cover his face, gasping and pretending to be scared.

Then Ollie broke in. "They're not wearing masks, you dope."

"Oh, excuse me," he said with mock politeness. "They look like masks to me."

This caused a roar of laughter from the whole gang. Jodie and Frannie would have run out of the store as fast as they could, but they were trapped. The boys were blocking the door.

"Yeah," chimed in another boy named Steve. "They look like two. . ."

Just then Tommy the Terrible shouted out, "Ah, lay off! We got no time to mess with girls. Get out of their way. We came to see Pete."

A curtain of silence fell on the whole group. As always, they did what Tommy said. The boys moved away from the door, and the two girls were forgotten as quickly as they could scoot outside. They didn't stop running till they were at the end of the block.

"Ow-w-w, let go!" Frannie whined. Jodie had been dragging her little friend along and was still squeezing her wrist in an iron grip.

"Sorry," Jodie said as she dropped the tiny wrist and breathed a big sigh of relief. She had not come that close to Tommy the Terrible since July, and she had almost forgotten what a pain he was, or rather, could be. That was the strange part. Today he had not been terrible. Just now he had saved the day.

Just then Jodie felt something warm and soft in her hand. She realized that while she gripped Frannie's wrist tightly with one hand, the other hand had clenched into a hard fist. As she opened her fist, she remembered the small, chocolate bar she had picked from Pete's basket and intended to eat later. Now, it was a squashed, gooey mess. Frannie laughed as Jodie licked the melted chocolate off the wrapper, getting it all over her fingers and face.

When they reached the end of Main Street, Jodie and Frannie set their meeting time for later that night and said goodbye. Jodie knew Mama would be worried if Jodie didn't get to the gin really soon, so she trotted all the way to make up time, only to find it was her turn to worry.

Mama wasn't there.

Mr. Carpenter, the owner of the gin, tried to tell Jodie what happened to Mama, something about coughing and fainting, but Jodie had only heard the word *sick*. Off she ran as fast as she could.

This was the beginning of a Halloween of nightmares.

When Jodie got home, there was a strange car in the driveway. Jodie's heart was pounding. What could have happened to Mama? Was she going to be all right? Who was here with her? A thousand questions raced through Jodie's mind as she burst through the kitchen door, stopped suddenly, and listened. Hearing voices coming from her mother's bedroom, Jodie inched quietly and slowly toward the bedroom door. She pushed Mama's door back ever so slightly and peeked in.

It was Dr. Porter. He was sitting on the edge of Mama's bed taking her pulse and doing all kinds of doctor things. There was a mask on Mama's face with a tube running into a strange-looking tank and another tube running from a bag into Mama's arm. Dr. Porter's helper, Nurse Ellen, was almost hidden in the shadow of the dark room as she worked busily. Jodie was horrified. She couldn't bear to see her mother like this and wanted to scream until it all went away.

"Mama!" Jodie called out. This outburst surprised everybody, even Jodie, who suddenly lost control. She ran to Mama's bed, grabbed Dr. Porter by the arm, and tried to push him away from her mother. Nurse Ellen jumped to his rescue as she took Jodie by the shoulders and pulled her back. Jodie could hear herself screaming, "No, no, leave my mother alone," but she did not know where the voice was coming from. Dr. Porter and his nurse both wrapped their arms around her as she kicked and screamed to get free. She wanted her mother, and she would not be stopped.

They would have wrestled her to the floor if Mama had not stopped the fight. Everyone froze when Mama lifted her head and reached her hand out to Jodie. The two adults let go of the hysterical child, and she dove to Mama's bed, burying her face in the sheet, sobbing, and pleading.

"Mama, don't be sick. *Please* don't be sick. I'll take care of you. Everything will be like it was before. Please, Mama, *please!*"

Mama lay motionless on the bed except to rest her weak fingers on Jodie's head and try to stroke her hair. She could not talk with the mask over her nose and mouth, but her eyes were telling Jodie that she loved her, and everything would be okay. Dr. Porter nodded to Nurse Ellen as a signal to let Jodie stay with Mama. Jodie knelt beside the bed, clutching the sheet with one hand and wrapping her other arm around her mother's thin body. She would stay there forever until Mama got well.

In a blink of an eye, it seemed to Jodie, her whole world had been turned upside down. And, in only a few minutes more, it would be flipped over again. There was a loud knock at the door. Jodie could hear an angry voice she did not recognize in the kitchen and footsteps in the hall; suddenly, the door to Mama's bedroom flew open. There stood Miss Rose Parker, the meanest woman Jodie ever knew, right here in her very own house in her mother's tiny bedroom.

Jodie remembered the cold, blue eyes that were now staring hard at her, so hard that they pierced right through her and made her shiver. Jodie clutched the sheet so tightly her fingernails dug deep into the mattress. She was terrified. And puzzled.

Jodie watched as the cold, blue eyes moved from her to the frail woman lying on the bed. She was amazed to see the eyes turn from anger to shock, then slowly and unexpectedly, to sadness. It was a heartbreaking kind of sadness that oozed to the surface from somewhere deep in her aunt's soul. This reaction puzzled Jodie even more than her aunt's appearance there that night. And now as Jodie stared at the eyes, she thought she could see tears welling up in them. It may have been the dimly-lit room or the tears in Jodie's own eyes. She would never know, for at that instant, Rose Parker disappeared from the room, taking Dr. Porter and Nurse Ellen with her and closing the door behind them.

As the three adults stood in the hall, their voices got louder as Miss Parker's anger returned. Jodie put all her energy into her ears to be able to hear what was being said. It was hard, but she could pick up a few words.

". . . someone let me know about Daisy?" Rose Parker was demanding of the doctor. ". . . long this has been going on? You should have. . ." Her voice was muffled as the pitch went up and down in her distress. The doctor simply muttered.

"Now, Miss Parker," and, "But, Miss Rose, you know. . . "It was all he could get in between the questions and the scolding.

Then the voices dropped to a whisper when her aunt asked, "What do you think, Bill?"

Jodie tried with all her might to hear what Dr. Porter was saying about her mother, but it was impossible. She was just about to let go of Mama and tiptoe to the door when it flew open again. Miss Parker came in alone and walked to Jodie, who was still kneeling by Mama's bed. To Jodie's surprise Miss Parker knelt down beside her and whispered, "Step out in the hall for a few minutes."

Miss Parker was so used to giving orders and having people jump to obey them that she was surprised when Jodie didn't budge from her mother's side. She hesitated a minute, then she stammered, "Jodie, isn't it?"

Jodie nodded without taking her eyes off Mama.

"I really need to talk to your mother," she added, beginning to wring her hands nervously. "Please. . .step outside. . .for just a few minutes."

Jodie still did not move.

"I promise I won't be long." Miss Parker certainly was not used to begging, and she was becoming more and more flustered. "Please." Then as if she had never said the word in her life, she added, "D-d-dear."

Jodie slowly turned to look at this strange woman and stare into the cold, blue eyes to see that they were filled with tears. Moving like a robot she stood up, clinging to the sheet and unable to step away from the bed. Miss Parker gently took Jodie by the arms and pulled her toward the door. Jodie unclenched her fist, and the sheet stayed in a wrinkled up ball beside Mama's hand.

"Maybe you can get something to eat," Miss Parker said as she led Jodie to the door. Dr. Porter and Nurse Ellen were standing in the hall, ready to burst into the bedroom at the first sound of trouble. Rose Parker eyed them both sternly, pushed Jodie toward them, and motioned with her head toward the kitchen.

Jodie had not even thought about the time or that she had not had dinner, or even that it was Halloween night. There would be no trick-or-treating for her, no scary masks, no soaping windows, no giggling and running away. She needed to let Frannie know, but there was no way she could leave this house, not even for a few minutes.

Nurse Ellen led Jodie down the hall and into the kitchen. As her eyes adjusted from the dark bedroom to the bright light of the kitchen, Jodie could see three figures sitting at the table. She was so confused. What was going on? Why were so many people in her house? To her surprise, it was Frannie, her mother, and, *oh my stars, it can't be but it is*, Mrs. Rutherford.

They stopped talking as soon as they realized she was in the room. The silence lasted only a few seconds, but it seemed longer to Jodie as she stared back at her unexpected guests. She didn't want all these people in her house. She didn't want everybody making such a fuss. Mama would be better tomorrow; she just needed a little rest and sleep. Jodie could take care of her mother like she always did, and they would both be fine.

"We brought you some supper, dear," Frannie's mother said as she scurried around to get a plate and fill it with food from dishes that were set out on the table.

Frannie didn't say a word but simply looked at Jodie in a pitiful way, part sadness and part guilt because she was wearing her Halloween costume. Jodie didn't say anything either but simply stared back. Frannie looked so strange in the big hoop earrings, bright red lipstick, and thick blue eye shadow her sister had gooped on her face that Jodie wasn't sure, at first glance, if it was her friend or not.

Jodie sat down at the table beside Mrs. Rutherford. She stared at the corn and peas and meatloaf and mashed potatoes that were piled high on her plate, but she wasn't a bit hungry. She was afraid even the smallest bite of food would stick in her throat and gag her. But everybody was staring at her, waiting to see her take a bite, and she knew she had to do it. As soon as she picked up her fork, Nurse Ellen left the room, and the two ladies began talking again. So Jodie picked at her supper as Frannie watched silently.

"I'm sorry about your mother," Frannie finally spoke up.

Jodie nodded. She felt a lump rise up in her throat and her eyes burn with tears. She managed to mumble, "She'll be better . . .tomorrow."

Frannie nodded in agreement.

Jodie pushed her plate away. She needed to get back to Mama. She thanked Frannie's mother and Mrs. Rutherford for the nice supper. To her surprise Mrs. Rutherford wrapped her big arms around Jodie and gave her a hug. Jodie allowed herself to sink into the soft, round body. It felt strange to be snuggled by her teacher, but it was warm and comforting. When she was finally released, Jodie turned to Frannie and gave her a little wave.

"Have fun," Jodie whispered.

Frannie lowered her head. She felt so guilty about going trick-or-treating without Jodie.

"You can have half of my candy," Frannie whispered back to ease the tension.

Jodie just nodded. She couldn't speak; she couldn't even smile. She only wanted to get back to her mother and hope everyone would just go away.

When she reached her mother's room, the door was closed. Miss Parker was still in the room with Mama. This made Jodie so angry that she wanted to break down the door and order her aunt to leave. Who did she think she was, coming into their house, taking over her place beside Mama? Her hands clenched into fists, and she would have pounded furiously on the door if it had not been for Dr. Porter.

"Jodie," he said softly, putting his arm around her shoulder. "Come sit with me for awhile."

Jodie didn't pull away but protested.

"No, I need to see about Mama."

"Sweetheart," the doctor spoke firmly. "Miss Rose is watching her. She'll be okay. Besides, we need to talk, just you and me."

Dr. Porter's voice was gentle but very serious. Something told Jodie she needed to hear what the doctor had to say. Maybe he would tell her how to help Mama get well. So she allowed herself to be led away from Mama to her own small room across the hall. Dr. Porter switched on the dim lamp beside her bed, and they sat down.

"Jodie," Dr. Porter began. His voice was still soft but now he sounded nervous as if he didn't know what to say. "You know your mother is very ill."

Jodie nodded, looking down at the floor, her fingers nervously twisting her dress in little knots.

"She's very, very ill," he repeated.

There was silence for a few seconds before he continued.

"I don't know if I can do much else for her."

Jodie felt the doctor tighten his hold on her shoulders. She began to tremble. This wasn't what he was supposed to tell her. He was a doctor; he was supposed to make Mama well.

"But, Dr. Porter," Jodie almost shouted. "Give her some medicine. She just needs to rest. She'll be better tomorrow. She can sleep all day. I can cook and clean the house and take care of her."

"Oh, I know you can do all those things," Dr. Porter gave her a squeeze. "You've been a big help to your mama. She's told me all about how hard you work."

Jodie looked up at the doctor in surprise. He tried hard to give her a smile, but he could only manage a sad, awkward one.

"You see, Jodie," he said. "Your mother's been coming to see me for quite a while now."

Jodie's eyes got even bigger. This was something Mama had never told her. Another one of Mama's secrets.

"She's been sick a long time, and we've been trying everything to make her better," Dr. Porter paused again. "Your mother, bless her heart, is worn out. Her body just can't fight it anymore."

Jodie stared at Dr. Porter. She wanted to scream. She wanted to pound on the doctor with her fists to make him say something different. She wanted to run to her mother and make her get up. But instead, Jodie's big, brown eyes filled with tears, and she fell into the doctor's chest. She did not want to cry in front of him but she couldn't help it. She cried loudly. She cried long and hard. Her whole body shook as the tears gushed.

Jodie wanted to hide in the doctor's white coat as he rocked and patted her gently. She wanted to stay there forever. She wanted everything outside this room to go away. But then, someone broke the spell. Someone was standing in the doorway of her room telling Dr. Porter to come. It was Miss Rose Parker.

The doctor quickly rose, laying Jodie carefully down on the bed. She wished she could crawl under the covers and bury her head in the pillow, wake up in the morning, and everything be like it was supposed to be. This was all a bad dream, the worse nightmare she had ever had, and as if in a dream, Jodie glided through her bedroom door and across the hall to her mother's bed.

There were people in the hall: Dr. Porter, Brother Stevens, Mrs. Turner, Rose Parker. She drifted past them without really seeing them, her eyes focused on the thin, pale figure lying on the bed. Everything was a blur. All sound was muffled. She was in a dream, and she wanted her mother to wake her up.

No one tried to stop her as she crawled up on the bed and lay down beside Mama. She was still sniffling from the hard cry, and her chest and shoulders jerked as she snuggled her face in Mama's neck and hair. Somehow she fell into a deep sleep.

At the first sign of dawn, when the night sky was brushed away with a faint pink light, and all was silent except for the whippoorwill calling to welcome the day, while Jodie slept, Mama died.

chapter ten

For the next three days, people came to Jodie's house. Some brought dishes of hot food, others carried flowers or fresh baked cakes. There was a lot of hugging, patting, and sobbing. The ladies dabbed their eyes with their handkerchiefs and said things like "Oh, you poor child," and "Bless your dear mother." Jodie was like a person under a spell. She could not talk or eat. She only stared blankly at the faces around her. When the house got too crowded and noisy, she would slip quietly out the kitchen door, sit on the porch, and think of all the times Mama and she had sat there together. Then she would drop her head into her lap and sob until her dress was wet, wishing her mother was there to stroke her hair.

Nighttime was the worst for Jodie. She would wake up screaming, soaking with sweat, kicking the covers, and calling out for Mama. Somewhere in the darkness she could feel a cool hand on her cheek. Sometimes there was a cup of water at her lips or a wet towel on her feverish head. Then she would fall back to sleep out of sheer exhaustion, only to wake again in a few hours.

On the third night, the last night Jodie would ever spend in her little house, something very strange happened. Mama came back.

As she did each night, Jodie was tossing and turning so hard in a fit of bad dreams that she screamed in her sleep and woke herself up. By the light of the full moon, she could see someone standing by the door—a woman with shoulder-length hair wearing a long nightgown.

"Mama?" Jodie cried out. "It's you! It's really you!"

The woman wrapped her arms around Jodie, rocking her gently.

"No, dear," she said. "No, I'm not your mama. I'm your aunt, your Aunt Rose."

She spoke so sweetly that for a moment Jodie felt warm and safe. Then the thought of her mother never coming back to hold her this way pierced her heart again and ripped open a floodgate of new tears. Aunt Rose held and rocked her till she cried herself to sleep again.

The next morning Jodie awoke to find Rose Parker sitting in a chair beside her bed. She looked like she had not slept a wink all night. She was pale with dark circles under her eyes, and the sight of her should have scared Jodie half to death. But somehow mean, old Miss Parker didn't look so mean anymore. There was a softness in her now that had not been there before. They stared at each other in the dim morning light, and both knew they had to face the day.

For this was the day they would say goodbye to Mama.

The day was only a big blur for Jodie—someone leading her here, sitting her down there, pushing food in front of her face, helping her into her best dress. She did not know what was happening or where she was going when they put her in a big black car with Miss Parker. The two rode in silence, sitting as far apart as possible against their opposite doors, staring out the windows.

Jodie knew she was entering her own small church, but she had never seen it so packed with people before. She could see the faces of people she knew—Frannie and her whole family, Mrs. Rutherford, even Pete from the drug store—but it was like a dream. As she walked with her aunt to the front row, she felt that all these people were just in her imagination, and they would all disappear any moment.

Brother Stevens was speaking, but Jodie only watched his lips move. Her ears were ringing, and her face was getting hot.

She felt dizzy and sick to her stomach. She couldn't bear to hear things said about her mother. She couldn't look at the wooden box covered in roses at the front of the church. This couldn't be happening. It couldn't be real. Jodie clenched her teeth together so hard her jaw popped, and she squeezed her eyes tightly together to keep the tears from flowing.

Before she knew what had happened the service had ended, and the big black car was pulling into the cemetery entrance. She recognized the tombstones that she had visited every Sunday for as long as she could remember. The car inched ever so slowly along the narrow road between the rows of graves. Like all the other Sundays, she looked for a small headstone with a tiny angel that simply read "infant." It always made her sad, but it was her favorite one. Jodie closed her eyes and pretended she was in the front seat beside Mama again. She knew that the car would stop in just a few seconds in front of her father's grave.

When she opened her eyes, she wasn't sure if it was her father's grave or not. There was dirt piled up high, covering most of the stone, and Jodie realized this was where her mother would be laid, right beside her father. For the first time Jodie felt something worse than the grief she had been suffering. She felt fear. A powerful, frightening, sickening fear gripped her body. And for the first time she thought of the word *orphan*.

For that was what she was. She had been grieving so hard for her mother, wishing everything would be like it was, wanting so badly to have her mother back, she had not even thought of what was to become of her after this day.

But she thought of it now. Who would live in her house with her? Would she be sent away to live with strangers? Or, worse yet, in an orphanage? All the sadness, the hurting, and the fear boiled up inside Jodie as she endured the last goodbye to her mother and watched the casket lowered into the ground. She could not breathe. Everything went black. With no warning Jodie fainted.

chapter eleven

When Jodie finally opened her eyes, she did not know where she was. It was dark except for the moonlight coming through the window. But it was not her window. She moved her arms and felt the cool soft sheet that covered her. This was not her bed.

Where was she? Jodie had no clue.

She sat up, rubbed her eyes, and looked around. She was in a large bed with four tall posts at each corner. The room was very large, and against the opposite wall, Jodie could see a pretty white dresser. There was a dressing table with a mirror next to the window that had ruffled curtains. She sat perfectly still for a long time, trying to figure out what was going on.

Could this be heaven? Jodie scratched her head through her matted hair. Had she died there beside Mama's grave? She had always thought heaven would be a bright and shiny place. And where were the angels?

She pinched the skin on her arm, and it hurt. She certainly didn't feel dead. No, this wasn't heaven. Then she thought of something else.

Had they already taken her to an orphanage? She looked around the beautiful room again and took a deep breath. It smelled of lavender or lilacs or one of those other wonderful scents she had only smelled when she and Frannie sniffed at the pretty perfume bottles in Pete's drug store. No, this couldn't be an orphanage, at least she didn't think so.

Just then Jodie heard footsteps, and the door to the room opened slightly. A thin ray of light fell on the bed. Jodie covered her eyes.

"Well, my, my, look-ie here," the voice said. "Look who's finally awake."

All Jodie could see was the black outline of a short, round woman standing in the light of the doorway. She waddled over to the bed, leaned over and put her small, rough hand on Jodie's head. When Jodie's eyes adjusted to the light, she could see that the woman's skin was dark. She had a large mouth with the whitest teeth Jodie had ever seen. The woman smiled as she studied Jodie's eyes and face.

"My name's Lucy," she said softly, still grinning. "And I got the best ham and cornbread you ever tasted waitin' on you in the kitchen."

She started to get up, then sat down again quickly. The bed shook with the sudden weight.

"Unless you're still feelin' poorly, then I'll bring a tray up here to you." She smiled and waited for Jodie to answer.

Jodie tried to speak, but her mouth and throat were so dry that nothing would come out. She cleared her throat and said hoarsely, "Where am I?"

"Why, child, you're in Miss Rose Parker's house," she seemed surprised that Jodie had asked such a question. "This here's your mama's old bedroom, when she's just a girl. Law-sy, it was a long time ago, but bless my soul, it do seem like only yesterday."

Jodie's tired expression did not change when she heard this, but inside she was churning with emotion. Mama's room. No wonder it was so pretty and smelled so nice. She wanted to touch everything in it. She wanted to feel close to her mother again.

But this room did not feel like her mother. Her mother was not the smell of lavender and lilacs, but freshly-ironed clothes and cotton and warm biscuits in the oven. Her mother was not a big, soft bed with pretty, white furniture and ruffled curtains. She was their old house and their old, small bedrooms with hardly any furniture at all. Jodie wanted to jump out of Miss Rose Parker's bed and run home, but her body would not even move to wiggle out from under the sheets.

"Now, about that food," Lucy said, getting back to business. "Do you want me to bring up a tray?"

"No, ma'am," Jodie replied in a whisper. "I'm getting up."

She was so weak from lack of food and sleep over the past several days that just getting to the edge of the bed was a struggle. Lucy's chubby hands gripped Jodie's arms and pulled her to her feet. Jodie leaned against Lucy's stout body and let herself be carried to the door. Lucy was not much taller than Jodie, but she was twice as round and strong as an ox.

When they stepped into the hallway, the view almost took Jodie's breath away. She was on the second floor, and through the banister rails she looked down at a sparkling chandelier hanging from the ceiling. The stairs curved around and widened at the base where they met a shiny marble floor. In the bright light Jodie could now see Lucy much better. Her skin was more than dark. It was almost black, and she wore a starched black dress with white cuffs and collar and a clean white apron on top. She was practically carrying Jodie down the stairs because Jodie was so busy looking around she forgot to step.

There were two rooms on each side of the entry hall. The walls of one room were covered with bookshelves all the way to the ceiling. Jodie had never seen so many books in one place in her whole life, not even in the school library. There was a huge oak desk beside a fireplace and a leather chair so big you could probably sink right into it and get lost.

The other room was a dining room with a long table that could seat about twelve people, a China cabinet that was filled with polished silver and crystal dishes, and a large picture of a woman sitting in a chair with a man standing by her side. They looked a lot like her grandparents in an old photograph of Mama's, the grandparents with the enormous tombstones.

Everything in the house looked clean and untouched, like nobody really lived there. All the furniture, the many pictures on the walls, the expensive rugs and vases were beautiful, but Jodie felt that it was all very cold, much like the owner of the house. She didn't like this house and hoped she could go home soon.

Then Lucy and Jodie entered the kitchen. It was bright and warm, and Jodie instantly fell in love with this room. It was twice as big as her old kitchen, but it had the same good smells and cozy feeling. There were pots and pans hanging from the ceiling, a long work table in the center, and a pantry filled with canned goods. There was a man with skin darker than Lucy's sitting at the table sipping on a glass of iced tea. His hair was peppered with gray, and he had on a starched white shirt with neatly pressed black pants. A black suit coat hung over the back of his chair, ready to be slipped on at a moment's notice. Lucy headed straight for the table and sat Jodie in a chair next to him.

"This here's William," Lucy said. The man grinned and showed the same white teeth as Lucy. Then she said to William,

"And this here's our new missus. . .Jodie."

With introductions done, Lucy quickly turned her back on them and headed to get a plate of warm food for Jodie.

"Nice to meet you, Miss Jodie," William said, grinning even bigger.

"It's just Jodie," she replied. "I'm not a Miss."

This made William chuckle. He shifted in his chair, took another sip of tea, and laughed again.

"You gonna be good for this house," he said. "Yes, ma'am, you just what this house needs."

Jodie wanted to ask what he meant by that, but she didn't get a chance, for, just then, Lucy was back and placed in front of Jodie a plate of hot, steaming ham, cornbread, peas, and boiled potatoes. Jodie realized how terribly hungry she was, and for the first time since before Halloween night, she dug in and stuffed her mouth full. This seemed to please her two new friends as they sat and watched her, both grinning from ear to ear.

When Jodie finally pushed the plate away, she wiped her mouth on the linen napkin Lucy had put in her lap. She looked at the two who had been watching her so closely and said, "Thank you. That was a fine meal."

97

Lucy and William looked at each other and grinned again. Then Lucy jumped up and whisked the plate away to clean up. Jodie was not used to anybody waiting on her. It was usually her job to clean the table and wash the dishes.

"I'll get that, Miss Lucy," Jodie started to get up. "I always wash the dishes for Mama at home."

Then, like a slap in the face, Jodie heard herself. For the past few minutes, sitting here with Lucy and William, she had forgotten her grief. But now it came flooding over her again. Mama was gone. Tears stung Jodie's eyes, and she looked away so William couldn't see. But he did see, and he knew what had happened. He stretched his long arm across the table and patted Jodie's shoulder, making her sit down again.

"It's alright, child," he soothed. "It's alright."

They sat in silence for a long time. Finally Lucy came back to the table, wiping her wet hands on her apron, and sat down with them again. Jodie had so many questions running through her head, but she couldn't seem to get any words out of her mouth.

Lucy was the first to speak. "We awfully glad you came to live with us."

Jodie could not hide the shock she felt on hearing this. It was as if she had poked her finger in an electric socket. And her voice trembled as she asked, "I'm going to live here? In this house? With Miss Parker?"

Lucy and William reflected the same surprise Jodie had just shown.

"Why, of course, dear," Lucy answered. "This here's family. Where else would you go? We the one's that love you. Miss Rose's your aunt, your flesh and blood. We gonna take real good care of you, you'll see."

"But. . .Miss Parker doesn't like me. . .or my mama," Jodie blurted out. "She's mean and hateful. And. . .and. . . I don't like her either."

By the look on the couple's faces, you would have thought Jodie just sprouted purple horns out of her head. Both mouths dropped open. They couldn't believe what they were hearing.

And for a moment they were speechless as Jodie's eyes filled with tears again.

Then Lucy broke through the silence and said, "Oh no, Miss Jodie," she said shaking her head. "Oh no, that ain't right at all, not at all. Why, Miss Rose loved your mama. She loved her dearly. And she loves you."

Lucy added, "We tried to get Miss Rose to come home. She needed to sleep, to get cleaned up, to rest, but, no sir-ree, she wouldn't leave you for a minute. Why, she still wouldn't rest until she knew you were going to be all right. Tucked you in bed herself tonight just after the doctor left. She's up in her room now, sound asleep. Bless her heart; she's just plain worn out."

Jodie listened in disbelief. Thinking about the past few days, she did remember someone being with her during the restless nights, but she didn't know it was her aunt. She now remembered the night she thought her mother had come back, only to learn it was Rose Parker. Remembering how her aunt looked the next morning, still sitting in the rocker where she had slept all night, Jodie was so confused. She did not know what to believe or how to feel. She was too tired to think about it, and it must have shown on her face.

"And look at you, child," Lucy said in a gentle voice, studying Jodie's face. "You just plain wore out, too. Let's get you back to bed. Things will look better in the morning. They always look better by daylight."

But things didn't look better in the morning.

Not the next morning. Not the whole next day. The only person Jodie saw all day long was Lucy, and she never even stopped to catch her breath as she buzzed around doing all sorts of jobs. William had driven Miss Rose into the city on some kind of business, so Jodie was left to roam around the big house all by herself. There were so many "delicates," as Lucy called them, sitting around that Jodie was afraid to touch anything for fear it would go crashing to the floor. She stared at the portraits on the walls, and the people in them seemed to stare right back. The house gave her a chilly, goose-bumpy feeling, so she went outdoors in the backyard.

The wind was cool, and the sky was gray and cloudy. The patio looked dreary with dead vines hanging from the latticework. The roses that were once so beautiful in the summer were gone. Jodie shivered as she walked around. She remembered the day she had accidentally come into this yard searching for the baseball. The memory chilled her more than the wind, so she went back indoors.

It was then she met Miss Sips. As Jodie walked through the door leading into the big library, a thin, gray and white paw swatted at her from behind the door. Jodie jumped and squealed, and the paw came out again, this time scratching her leg. Jodie sat down on the floor, trying to catch her breath and figure out what had just attacked her. Slowly, she peeked around the door, and the paw came flashing out at her again. Jodie was quicker this time, jerking her head back just in time to escape the tiny claws. She got a good look at the creature, though, and realized it was the same gray and white cat that had jumped in the window one Sunday morning, scaring her half to death.

Jodie sat very still, waiting for another attack. It didn't come, so she called to the cat, "Here, kitty, kitty." But the cat stayed hidden behind the door. By the fireplace, Jodie saw a small, fuzzy ball with a bell on it. It was one of Miss Sips favorite toys. Jodie crawled to get the ball then sneaked up to the door. She jangled the bell and thumped the ball on the floor. Miss Sips sprang from her hiding place and pounced on the toy, making Jodie squeal with laughter. The cat hissed at Jodie, scratched her on the nose, and darted out of the room. Jodie frowned and rubbed her nose. Maybe she and Miss Sips wouldn't be friends after all.

Jodie finally saw her Aunt Rose that night at dinner. To Jodie's disappointment the plates and serving dishes were placed on the formal dining table instead of the smaller one in the kitchen. She felt small and uncomfortable sitting across from her aunt at one end of the long table. All day a thousand questions had raced through Jodie's head, and she had been impatient for her aunt to come home so she could get some answers. But now, Jodie could not bring herself to say anything at all. They both sat in silence, taking small pecks at their food and chewing quietly.

Finally, Aunt Rose cleared her throat and said, "Did you have a nice day, Jodie?"

This startled Jodie, and she choked down the spoonful of mashed potatoes she had just put in her mouth before answering, "Yes, ma'am."

Aunt Rose simply nodded.

This broke the ice for Jodie, and she got up her nerve to ask, "Today is Monday, isn't it?"

Aunt Rose looked calmly at Jodie, nodded and answered, "Yes, it's Monday."

"I was supposed to go to school today," Jodie said flatly.

This seemed to surprise Aunt Rose. She straightened her shoulders, dabbed her lips with a napkin, and stared at Jodie. This reaction worried Jodie, but it also helped to give her courage to ask the next question.

"Do I. . .do I still get to go to school?" she almost whispered. "I mean. . .my school?"

Aunt Rose still didn't answer, and Jodie began to squirm. The questions she had began to rise up in her like boiling water in a pot, and without warning, they bubbled up and overflowed right out of her. Her voice got louder as she blurted out, "Do I have to go to a new school? Are you going to send me away? To an orphanage? What about my house? Who will live in my house? Who will look after our things?"

Jodie's face had become blood-red from her outburst. Her brown eyes were large and round with the panic that she felt inside. She finally paused to catch her breath, and Aunt Rose took this chance to break in.

"Jodie. . .dear. . .please," she reached over and put her hand on Jodie's trembling one. "Listen to me. You're not going anywhere. You're going to stay right here. . .in my house." She patted Jodie's hand.

"And yes, you will go to school," she assured her. "Your old school."

Her aunt's eyes were sad and seemed to be pleading with Jodie not to be scared or worried. This made Jodie feel ashamed that she had lashed out. Embarrassed, Jodie looked down at her place but didn't eat another bite.

"I wasn't sure if you were well," Aunt Rose continued. "To go to school, that is." She hesitated, then added, "I'm not sure now if. . .if . . . you're ready."

Aunt Rose fidgeted with her silverware. "You know, Jodie, you don't have to go back until you think you're ready. I've already spoken with Mrs. Rutherford, and she wants you to take your time. She'll help you catch up on your work whenever you come back."

Jodie could only stare in disbelief. She sat in silence a moment, letting it all soak in. When she finally spoke it was just a whisper, "You talked to my teacher? Mrs. Rutherford?"

Aunt Rose smiled. "Yes. As a matter of fact, I went to your school today. Mrs. Rutherford and I have known each other a very long time." She gave a little chuckle and smoothed the tablecloth with her fingertips. "This may seem hard to believe, but Mrs. Rutherford was once my teacher, too. Ages ago. But I wouldn't be surprised if she's still using the same old wooden ruler. My, that was an attention-getter."

Aunt Rose looked at Jodie, and their eyes met. They both smiled, thinking of how Mrs. Rutherford could slant that ruler right under your nose, making you shake all over. It was hard to picture her aunt as a little girl, sitting in one of those small desks, trying to listen. But then, Jodie remembered the day Mrs. Rutherford talked about her mama. Of course, Aunt Rose and Mama would have gone to the same school and had the same teachers. Jodie felt a sudden warmth come over her. She liked the feel of her aunt's hand on hers, and she liked the eyes that were now soft and smiling at her. She soaked up this good feeling before she said, "I'd like to go to school tomorrow."

Aunt Rose sighed. "Are you sure? There's no hurry."

"Yes, ma'am, I'm sure," she answered. "Really. I'd like to go tomorrow."

"Well then, young lady," Aunt Rose put her napkin on the table and stood up. "You'll need to get in bed."

Jodie put her napkin on the table just as her aunt had done and stood up, too.

"Oh, by the way," her aunt added as she turned to leave. "I did some shopping today. You should find everything you'll need for school in the closet in your room." She stopped at the door and looked at Jodie. "Goodnight, dear. Have a good sleep."

And that was just what Jodie did. For the first time in almost a week Jodie slept without having nightmares. But before she drifted off to sleep, she lay thinking about all the things her aunt had said. This was her new home. She wiggled under the covers of her bed. She would never get used to this four-poster bed. She would never like eating at the long dining table or passing by the portraits of people she didn't know. She would never feel at home in this big, cold house.

Then she thought of going to school the next day. She missed Frannie and the other girls. She even missed Mrs. Rutherford, and the thought of seeing them again made her feel good. Everything in her life had changed, everything, that is, except school. She could count on that.

At least that's what Jodie believed as she drifted off to sleep. The next day would prove her wrong.

chapter twelve

It was as if a blanket of ice had fallen over Jodie's classroom. Everyone froze as she stepped inside the door. Even Mrs. Rutherford stopped writing on the chalkboard to watch Jodie. She stared back at the nineteen pairs of eyes that were all staring at her. This was not what she expected at all. Her happy return to school was *not* going right.

In fact, nothing so far that day had gone right. She didn't want to ride to school in the big black car, and when she found out at breakfast that William would drive her, she hurried like anything to be early so no one would see her. But William was as slow as a mud turtle, and by the time they arrived at school, Jodie could see all her classmates' faces glued to the classroom window watching them. To make things even worse, the mud turtle suddenly became a jack rabbit and had the car door open for her before she could get out by herself.

So there she stood in her new blue wool jumper, knee socks, and shiny new black patent shoes that her aunt had bought for her, enduring the silence. It wasn't so much that Jodie looked any different or acted any differently, but the other children did not know what to say to a little girl who had just lost her mother or how to treat a friend who was not poor like them anymore. Even Frannie did not know what to say to her best friend, so she just stood there like the others staring at Jodie. Thank goodness, Mrs. Rutherford finally broke the ice by walking over to Jodie and putting her arm around her shoulder. All the other students let out a breath and continued on to their desks. Their teacher spoke a few soft words of welcome that only Jodie could hear and then went back to her boardwork.

Jodie felt like a stranger in her own classroom. She moved awkwardly toward Frannie, who was still looking down at Jodie's brand new shoes. She wanted so badly to talk to Frannie away from everyone else. There was so much to tell her. But all she could say was "hi."

Frannie peeked up at Jodie over her black-rimmed glasses. She had a strange look on her face, a worried look, almost scared. It seemed like a forever-long time that the two friends faced each other in silence, and they might never have moved if Mrs. Rutherford's voice hadn't jarred them into motion. It was time to start class. As Jodie stepped past Frannie toward her desk, Frannie whispered very quietly, "Are you a rich girl now?"

Then Frannie lowered her head and headed quickly for her desk.

Jodie was shocked and embarrassed. Is that what everyone was thinking? She sunk into her desk. And to make things even worse, there was a note on the top of her desk. She picked it up and looked around to see if anyone was watching her. All eyes were on Mrs. Rutherford. Jodie slid the note into her lap and slowly unfolded the paper. She was almost afraid to look at it. And when she did, she wished she hadn't. Her breathing stopped, and her face got red hot with embarrassment. The note said:

I'm sorry about your mother.

Tommy White

She quickly looked around again to see if anyone had seen her read the note. Everyone had eyes glued to a page in the math book. Jodie quickly stuffed the note in her pocket, scrambled to find her math book, and thumbed the pages frantically to catch up. The strangest thing was that Mrs. Rutherford didn't scold Jodie for not paying attention. The teacher didn't call on Jodie all day or slam the ruler down when she daydreamed, not the whole livelong day. It seemed like everyone was walking on egg shells around her, and by the end of the day, Jodie was ready to explode.

She burst through the door of the kitchen, startling Lucy so badly that she dropped a bowl of peas, and they scattered on the floor in all directions. Jodie dropped her books on the table with a loud bang, sat down, and slammed her elbows on the table. She dug the palms of her hands into her eye sockets to hold back the angry tears that wanted to break loose all day.

Just then William came in the back door. Lucy looked to him for help, but all he could do was shrug his shoulders. Neither one knew what in the world was going on or what to do about it.

"Law-aw-sy, child," Lucy said as she placed a plate of fresh-baked cookies on the table in front of Jodie. In her other hand she was holding a glass of cold milk. "What in heaven's name is troubling you so?"

Jodie jabbed her palms even deeper into her face and refused to look up. William and Lucy sat down at the table, shaking their heads, and looking at each other in a pitiful, puzzled way. They watched Jodie as if she might explode right in front of them. Finally William spoke up.

"You know, Miss Jodie," he said. "I don't know much about school. I quit going once I got about your age. But, seems to me, it wasn't as bad as all that. And your school. . .well. . .your school looks to be a real nice place to go. As I recall just this morning, somebody was real happy to be going back. . .if I recall right."

William cut his eyes toward Lucy and smiled. She nodded, smiled back and added, "As I recall, just this morning, *somebody* was telling me right here at this here table, how she couldn't *wait* to see her friends and her nice teacher again."

Jodie's shoulders relaxed. She slid her hands away from her eyes and placed them on each side of her head. Her eyes and face were red from the pressure, but she still did not look up.

"That's right," William continued to prod Jodie into speaking. "They the nicest folk at that school you ever want to know. Why, I'd sure 'nough like to go there myself."

Jodie could stand it no longer.

"That's just the problem," she blurted out. "Everybody's too nice. Even Mrs. Rutherford. She didn't slam her ruler on my desk. Not once today. And Frannie. . .she's supposed to be my best friend. All she did was stare at me and make a fuss about carrying my books, and everybody fought over sitting by me at lunch."

She jammed her hand into her pocket and brought out the note.

"And look what Tommy the Terrible put on my desk. What does he think he's doing, anyway?"

William and Lucy read the note and looked at each other, even more puzzled than ever.

Jodie paused to catch her breath. She had worked herself up into a state of outrage. William and Lucy stared at her with wide eyes. They still did not grasp the problem. Jodie saw their confused looks.

"You don't understand," she tried to explain. "School's not supposed to be different." Tears began to roll down her face. "I'm not different. I'm not a rich girl. I'm not an orphan." She started to cry hard. "I just want everything to be like it's supposed to be."

She folded her arms on the table, put her head down on them and sobbed.

"I want to go home. I want my mama."

Lucy jumped up and wrapped her arms around Jodie. Neither William nor Lucy could bear to see the girl so upset. Lucy pulled Jodie into her lap and began to rock her. Jodie's legs were so long that her feet touched the floor, and she had trouble staying on the round woman's lap. Though Jodie knew she was too old to be rocked like a baby, she didn't care. Listening to Lucy's soft humming, Jodie thought about school. She didn't think she could bear another day being treated like a China doll.

She finally sat up and asked, "What am I going to do?"

Lucy helped Jodie back into her chair and straightened her apron.

"Well, I'll tell you what you do," Lucy smiled, showing her pearly white teeth. "You just be you. And 'fore you know it,

108

everything will be back the way it's supposed to be. You'll see, everything in its own good time."

And that's just what happened. Each day got a little better. Frannie quit staring at Jodie's new clothes and started acting like her best friend again. All the other girls quit paying so much attention to her, and even Mrs. Rutherford stared at her over the rim of her glasses when she wasn't on the right page. William made sure she was at school early and let her get out of the car by herself. Time was working everything out. And before Jodie knew it, school was letting out for Christmas vacation.

By now, Jodie had gotten used to the routine of her new home. Breakfast in the kitchen with Lucy and William. Dinner in the formal dining room with Aunt Rose. She never had too much to talk about with her aunt. The room was always so quiet, and other than asking Jodie about her day, Rose Parker didn't have much to say either.

But on the night of her last day of school before Christmas break, both aunt and niece were very talkative. There had been a party at school, and Jodie was telling her aunt all about it. She could name every gift Mrs. Rutherford got from each of her students. Jodie described with great delight the look on her teacher's face when she opened Jodie's gift. Aunt Rose had bought Mrs. Rutherford a set of monogrammed linen hand towels, very pretty and delicate. This seemed to please Aunt Rose that the gift had been a big hit. She smiled and then startled Jodie by asking, "What do you want for Christmas, Jodie?"

For a few seconds Jodie was stunned. She had not thought about Christmas gifts for herself. In the past she had always known exactly what she wanted for Christmas, a new baseball and glove or a new baseball bat. There had never been enough money to buy either of those things, so she always ended up getting new mittens or a scarf that her mother had knitted, a new pair of shoes, or a new winter coat.

Yes, in the past, she would have answered right away. But that was before she swore off baseball for life. Now she didn't know what to say; she didn't know what she wanted.

Aunt Rose reached over and patted Jodie on the knee.

"You just think about it for a while. You can let me know later."

But Jodie never did. She was too busy helping Lucy and William get ready for Christmas. They decorated the house with evergreen and lights and pretty red bows. She helped William pick out a tree in a nearby forest and watched as he chopped it down. They brought it home and set it up in the big living room next to the window. William held Jodie up as she placed a beautiful angel on the top of the tree, and even Aunt Rose helped to put the ornaments and lights on it. Miss Sips swiped at the colorful balls as Aunt Rose and Jodie hung them on the tree and swiped at Jodie if she got too close. Lucy served hot chocolate and tea cakes as they worked. When they were finished it was the most beautiful tree Jodie had ever seen.

She was also very busy making a gift for Aunt Rose. Lucy was teaching Jodie how to embroider, and she was trying to finish a handkerchief before Christmas morning. It was a close race to the deadline, but despite her sore, needle-pricked fingers, she won the race. By Christmas morning the gift was finished, wrapped, and placed under the tree.

To Jodie's surprise there were several gifts for herself under the tree. She sat and stared at the pretty packages. Aunt Rose sat in her big Victorian chair with Miss Sips in her lap waiting for Jodie to unwrap her gifts.

"Well, go on, dear," she urged. "After all, it is Christmas. It's time to open."

Jodie didn't know where to begin. She picked a medium-sized present with a big red bow and carefully pulled off the wrapping paper. Lifting the box lid, she found a matching hat, scarf, and mittens. This gift made her think of her mother, but it was Christmas, and she did not want to be sad. She looked up at Aunt Rose, smiled, said "thank you," and closed the box. Then Jodie opened up two more small presents; one was a nightgown, and the other was a doll that had the face of an angel and a pretty velvet dress.

Jodie was thrilled over her gifts, but not as thrilled as she would be when she opened the next one. She couldn't believe her eyes! It was a spotless, white baseball sitting in the palm of a brand-new baseball glove. Pulling them out of the box, she lifted them to her face. She wanted to smell the leather and feel the smoothness. Suddenly she forgot that she hated baseball; she

forgot that she was never going to play the game again. All she wanted to do was hug the ball and glove to her chest.

She turned to Aunt Rose with eyes as big as saucers.

"How did you know?" she asked. "How did you know?"

Aunt Rose's eyes were twinkling with delight. She smiled. Jodie had never seen her face look so soft, so happy, so much like her mother's face.

"Your mother kept a diary," she said softly. "I found it among her things. She wrote how you love baseball. She was sad because she couldn't buy you the ball and glove."

Jodie still couldn't believe she was holding her very own baseball, and she kept rubbing her hands over it. Aunt Rose watched and smiled.

"I think your mother would be happy to see you right now," she added.

"Oh, thank you, thank you," Jodie gushed.

"But, dear, you have one more gift, a very *special* gift," Aunt Rose said, pointing under the tree. "Over there, that small one."

Jodie didn't think any gift could be more special than what she had already gotten, but she picked up the package and carefully unwrapped it. At first, she didn't know what it was. It was old and used and worn-out looking. It was some sort of book. Aunt Rose saw the puzzled look on her face, and she asked Jodie to bring the book over to her. Lifting Miss Sips off her lap, she gently lowered the cat to the floor. She patted the chair for Jodie to share the seat with her. Jodie had never been this close to her aunt before, and it felt awkward. But she was very curious to know about the book.

Aunt Rose sighed as she took the book from Jodie's hands. She ran her fingers over the cover and looked at it sadly. Jodie thought she might cry but instead she said, "This belonged to your mother, Jodie. It was her diary."

Aunt Rose looked at Jodie for a very long time. She looked so sad that Jodie felt sad, too.

"It's not the same one where I read about your love of baseball. This is a very old diary. Daisy started this diary when she was only seventeen."

Aunt Rose looked away. The room was silent except for the crackling of the fireplace. Aunt Rose stared into space, and her eyes became moist. Jodie wanted to shake her and tell her everything was okay, but she sat quietly and waited.

"I want you to have this," she continued. "I want you to read it. You may not understand some of it, or all of it, but I think you're old enough to know more about your mother. . .and your daddy, your family. . .and. . .and me."

Jodie looked at the book again, this time her heart was beating fast. This book held the secrets she had always wanted to know. The things that her mother would never talk about. The things her mother always said Jodie would understand when she was older. And here was her aunt, giving her the secrets, believing she was old enough now to know.

Aunt Rose gave the diary back to Jodie, who took it as if it were a precious jewel and held it to her chest. She would read it. She would discover her mother. She would learn the secrets of the Sunday rose.

Jodie looked up and saw a tear roll down her aunt's cheek.

"Thank you," Jodie whispered.

chapter thirteen

Jodie sat cross-legged on her bed and stared at the old diary in her lap. The edges of the leather binding were ragged. Gold lettering that said *My Diary* had long since worn off. Jodie ran her fingers over the cover for the hundredth time. Two days had passed since she had unwrapped the precious present, and she had not read a page of it yet. She had flipped through the pages and looked at her mother's girlish handwriting, but something had stopped her from reading the words she had written. It was a feeling of stepping off a cliff into the unknown. The fear of what was ahead had kept Jodie from finding out.

But now she was ready. She opened the book and took her first step into the past. The first page was dated May 7, 1939. Jodie recognized this date as her mother's birthday. Mama had received the diary as a present on her seventeenth birthday, and the first entry told all about a special dinner with Daddy (Jodie's grandfather), Rose, and a few friends. It must have been a very happy day for Mama. Jodie could almost feel Mama's excitement jump off the page.

Jodie smiled as she turned page after page, stepping into her mother's world as a young girl. It seemed strange that Mama had such carefree thoughts. She rattled on about silly things, friends and school, who was wearing what or who had a new boyfriend or going shopping. It didn't sound like the mother

Jodie knew at all, the woman who always worried and seemed sad on the inside.

Jodie read eight pages before she finally looked up. She realized the sun was going down, and her room was getting dark. Rubbing her eyes, she closed the book. She fell back onto the pillows, and for a long time she thought about her mother. Then she thought about Aunt Rose. How strange everything was! Her aunt had been nothing but nice to her so far, but there was something about Aunt Rose that Jodie didn't trust. She couldn't believe Rose Parker was a kind and loving person when she had hated Mama so much. Jodie thought about how Mama had brought a rose to this very house every Sunday, how they had to sneak around and hide from Miss Parker. Never once did her aunt talk to them, or visit them, or even say "thank you" when Mama was alive.

Jodie was awakened by a voice. She must have dozed off and had no idea how long she had been sleeping. The bedroom was totally dark now. She sat up. For a few seconds she did not know where she was. She heard the voice again. It was Lucy calling her to dinner. Jodie smiled. She had been in the middle of the nicest dream about Mama. But then she realized it was only a dream, and the deep sadness that she had felt so many times in the past months flooded over her again.

The next day Jodie settled down in the big leather chair in the library to read some more of Mama's diary. So far she had read nothing of any importance except that she could guess her grandfather must have been a very strict father. Mama talked about his rules and the way he constantly forbade his two daughters to do this and that. There was no mention of Jodie's grandmother in the diary, and Jodie decided to ask Aunt Rose about her at dinner.

Jodie read only two pages when she looked out the window and saw snow beginning to fall. It was the first snow she had seen since last January, and she would love to run around in it. She was just about to close the diary when something at the bottom of the page dated May 18, 1939, caught her eye. She saw the name John Mills, a name she saw every Sunday on her daddy's headstone on Cedar Hill. She suddenly forgot about the snow and began reading the page:

Dear Diary,

Tonight was very exciting. Rose went to her senior prom. She had on the most beautiful dress you ever saw. It was white with red roses on the waist and the shoulder. She looked so pretty and was so excited. Even Daddy smiled when he saw her. Then he preached to her about being a lady and all that stuff. Everyone was running around trying to get her ready. But when her date came to the door we waited upstairs so Daddy could talk to him. It was John Mills. Poor thing. He looked really nervous talking to Daddy. John was probably getting the same speech about being a gentleman. He looked relieved when Rose finally came down the stairs to rescue him. Rose is so lucky to be going to the prom.

P.S. John is tall. He has dark brown hair and very dark brown eyes. Very handsome.

Jodie looked up from the diary with a surprised and confused look on her face. Her eyes stared at the staircase and the hallway just outside the library door. She tried to imagine the scene that night. A tall young man waiting anxiously for his date as he listened politely to a very stern father. A young Rose Parker drifting down the stairs in a pretty white prom dress. A younger Mama watching from a hiding place somewhere at the top of the stairs. It was almost more than she could imagine, and so very strange to think that her aunt had gone to the prom with her daddy.

Jodie forgot about the snow. She was glued to the writing in the diary, flipping the page and reading again. The next three pages described the last days of the school year. Mama told about a picnic and going swimming in the creek with friends and other silly things. There was no mention of John Mills or Rose or the prom, and Jodie was disappointed. She scanned the next few pages looking for names until she found a page with the initials J.M. and she began to read:

July 11, 1939

Dear Diary,

We had the most fun today. Daddy had his yearly barbeque in the backyard. There were a whole lot of people here. Mary and Jenny came. We played croquet with Matthew Logan and his cousin, Bob, from St. Louis. The girls won. It was fun. Some boys had firecrackers left over from the Fourth. Daddy let them shoot them in the front yard. Mr. Banks brought his guitar, and his wife brought her fiddle. We sat around and sang songs and ate ice cream until it got dark. J.M. came and sat in the swing with Rose. He would probably hold her hand if Daddy didn't watch him like a hawk. He played one game of croquet with us. The boys won that one. But it was still fun.

The next entry was August 3, 1939. As Jodie read, she could sense that something was troubling Mama. It wasn't so much in the words she wrote, but there was a difference in the way she said things.

Dear Diary,

Nothing to do today. Rose went shopping. Didn't feel like going with her. She'll be going away to State College in a few weeks. I wish I were going away. Went to the movies last night with Sue Ellen. She met her new boyfriend, Hank, and left with him. Thank goodness J.M. was there. He drove me home in his truck. We talked about Rose and college. He's not going to college this year. He has to work in his father's hardware store. That's too bad, but he doesn't seem to mind.

I like his smile.

September 6, 1939

Dear Diary,

Rose left for college today. We sat up almost all night talking. Mostly about J.M. She's in love with him. She's going to miss him terribly. Daddy wants her to go to college at least two years, but she hopes they can get married after that. She hopes he'll give her an engagement ring for Christmas. J.M. came by to see her off. Rose gave him a hug and began to cry. That made Lucy cry, and then I cried. We almost made Daddy cry. I hope I find someone just like J.M. He gave me a wink when he left.

September 8, 1939

Dear Diary,

School has started again. I like my teachers, except Mrs. Crump, English. She made me sit on the front row. I don't think she likes me. I wish I were old enough to go to State College like Rose. I don't think I can wait one more year. I wish I could move away from home now. It would be so much fun. I miss Rose already. She won't be home until Thanksgiving. Daddy says maybe we can visit her before then. She promised to write me. Jim Webb asked me to the dance on Friday, but I don't want to go with him. I wish he'd leave me alone.

November 1, 1939

Dear Diary,

I know it's been a long time since I've written. So much has happened. School is okay. I have a lot of work to do. Last night was Halloween. A bunch of us rode around in Wilson H.'s car. It was fun. We went to the lake and built a

*fire. J.M. was there. He seems to be everywhere
I go. We sat and talked for a long time. I
don't know what is happening. He held my
hand. I like him so much. I wish Rose would
have a new boyfriend when she comes home.
Everything is so mixed up. I feel good and bad
at the same time. I just have to stop talking to
J.M. Everything will be back to normal when
Rose comes home for Thanksgiving.*

November 21, 1939

Dear Diary,

*Rose comes home in three days. I don't know if
I can face her. Something terrible has happened.
J.M. kissed me. I don't know how I let that
happen. It just did. One minute we were
talking, and the next minute he was looking
into my eyes. He has such beautiful, brown
eyes. Before I knew it he was kissing me. I
won't ever see him again. Rose will never ever
find out. I would rather die than hurt her. I
love my sister more than I will ever love a boy.
But I think I do love him.*

Jodie slammed the diary shut; she had read enough and
was more confused than ever. So many different feelings were
building up inside her. She was angry and hurt and sad. It
seemed so sneaky for Mama to betray her sister like that, and
Jodie didn't want to believe it. She was angry with her daddy
for causing so much trouble. She was beginning to feel sorry
for Aunt Rose after all this time thinking she was the mean one.
Maybe Mama had been right all along. Maybe Jodie wasn't old
enough to understand this yet.

Jodie looked out the window and watched the snow fall.
The big library was cold, and she wished she had her big quilt
from off her bed upstairs. Shivering, she did not get up. She
didn't want to see or talk to anybody right now. She didn't want
to think about all that stuff in the diary. She wished Frannie was

here so they could play together in the snow. She wished she was at her old house so she could run and get Frannie.

And then, Jodie's wish came true. There was a knock on the door, and when Lucy opened it, there stood Frannie and her brother, Ralph. They had walked all the way from their house in the snow to see Jodie, who couldn't believe her eyes! She stuffed the diary in the seat of the big, leather chair and ran to get her coat. She would never tell Frannie about the diary. She didn't want her to know what her parents had done. She would never talk about it with any living soul.

It was the most fun day Jodie could remember in a long time. They built a snowman and a snow fort, had a snowball war, and ran around till their faces and noses were blood red from the cold. Lucy fixed them hot chocolate and sandwiches for lunch. Then they were off again with cardboard boxes for sledding on the hill down the street. Jodie wanted the day to last forever.

When it was finally time for them to go home, William warmed up the big black car. Frannie's eyes got big as she sat down in the backseat. Jodie laughed at the sister and brother who seemed so excited about riding in her aunt's car. They had spent most of the day with their mouths open in awe of everything around them. Now that Frannie had overcome her fear of Jodie's new house and family, she promised to come and see her again.

That night at dinner Aunt Rose couldn't help noticing Jodie's good mood.

"The snow was beautiful, wasn't it?" she commented.

"Yes, ma'am," Jodie answered happily. "And fun too."

Then Jodie told her aunt about Frannie and Ralph and all the fun things they had done.

"You know, Jodie," Aunt Rose said. "You can have your friends over whenever you like. This is your house, too."

Jodie smiled. Somehow the anger about the diary and the confused feelings about life itself that she had felt earlier melted away like the snow on her boots. For the first time, she began to feel like she could have a life in this house. She glanced up at the portrait of her grandparents.

"Will you tell me about my grandmother?" Jodie asked softly.

"What?" Aunt Rose was surprised. She saw Jodie looking at the picture. "Oh. Of course, dear. What would you like to know about her?"

"Everything."

Aunt Rose seemed flustered and didn't know what to say.

"Well. . .let's see," she began. "Your grandmother's name was Lily Mae Winchester. She was born in a small town near Savannah, Georgia. She met my father at an auction. He was helping his father, your great-grandfather, buy horses. She and my father were married a few months later, and she moved to Greenwood with him. He built this house for her."

Aunt Rose looked up at the portrait. "You know, she was a beautiful woman. Your mother looked a lot like her." She looked back at Jodie and smiled. "Almost exactly like her."

Aunt Rose was finished. She sat back and sighed.

"When did she die?" Jodie asked. "How old were you?"

Aunt Rose's eyes were fixed on Jodie's face. She waited a few seconds and then answered, "She died when I was fourteen. She was sick for a very long time."

Aunt Rose lowered her eyes and dabbed them with her napkin. Her voice was weak when she spoke again.

"Losing our mother was very much like you losing your mother. There was nothing we could do. Nothing. And I'm sure that's why your mother never told you how sick she was. There was nothing you could do." Aunt Rose wiped her eyes again. She whispered to herself, "I only wish I had known."

Then she got up quickly and left the room. Jodie felt bad that she had made her aunt remember. She sat in the big dining room all by herself for a while, then she walked quietly to the library and dug the diary out of the cushion. Heading upstairs for bed, she knew she would not read any more of the diary tonight. But she did have one more thing to do before she went to sleep.

Jodie carried the new ball and glove down the hall to her aunt's bedroom. She held them to her nose one more time and took a deep sniff. Then she laid them on the floor by the door. She had no need for the present. It was only right to give it back.

chapter fourteen

Next morning, Jodie was up bright and early. Christmas vacation was over, and it was time to go back to school. After spending the day with Frannie, Jodie was excited about seeing her friends. Dressing quickly in her black stockings, she thought of how her mama hated to see her torn stockings. But that was when she played baseball. Things were different now. These stockings would last a long time.

Jodie went down to the kitchen, which was the warmest room in the house. She settled down at the small table and waited for her breakfast. Lucy was humming as she kneaded the biscuit dough.

"My, you up awful early this morning," she said with a big smile.

Jodie just nodded. She wasn't much of a talker this early in the morning.

Just then the door leading from the hallway burst open. Jodie jumped, and Lucy nearly dropped her pan of biscuits. It was Miss Rose, and Miss Rose rarely entered the kitchen unless she had some important business to discuss with Lucy or William. She always had her breakfast delivered on a tray to her study. Both Lucy and Jodie stared at the woman standing there in her robe and slippers. She was holding the ball and glove in her hand.

"Jodie, why was your ball and glove outside my door?" she asked.

Jodie looked like she'd been caught with her hand in the cookie jar. She lowered her eyes and answered shyly.

"I'm giving them back."

"But why?" Aunt Rose seemed so distressed over such a little thing.

Jodie looked up. She felt badly that she had upset her aunt, but she had to be truthful.

"I don't play baseball anymore," she stated flatly.

Staring at Jodie, Aunt Rose seemed so confused and hurt, and it surprised Jodie. Why should her aunt care whether she played baseball or not? It didn't make sense.

"But. . .but, I thought you loved baseball," Aunt Rose stammered. "Your mother wrote that you did. And. . .and you're good at it. Really good. I saw for myself that you could knock a ball over a fence. Don't you remember that day in my backyard?"

Jodie was shocked. She didn't know if her aunt had recognized her or even remembered that day. She couldn't deny that she had hit the ball, and yes, she *was* good at it. And she *did* love baseball. But not anymore.

Jodie took a deep breath and began her tale. Once she got started she was off like a freight train. She ranted about how useless it was to keep playing baseball. It was a boys' game. And boys were stupid and mean and stingy. Aunt Rose slipped into the chair beside Jodie at the table as she listened. Lucy was working busily with her hands, but her ears were glued to Jodie.

Then Jodie got started on the horrible events of the little league try-outs. By this time William had come in from clearing snow from the sidewalk, and he tuned his ears onto Jodie's story, too. Somewhere between Tommy the Terrible's attack on her in the road and getting dressed at Frannie's that fateful Saturday morning, the biscuits baked and were laid out on the table along with strawberry jam and bacon and grits.

No one said a word as Jodie described the scene at the try-outs. Aunt Rose motioned to Lucy and William to sit down with them, and sometime during the big hit, the home run, and the fatal slip of the baseball cap, they ate breakfast. When Jodie finished her story, everyone sat in silence. William was shaking his head at the injustice.

Lucy simply said, "My, my, *my* child. That ain't right. That just ain't right."

And Aunt Rose was the strangest of all. She continued to stare at Jodie as she had done throughout the entire story. Then her head began to nod as if she were thinking about something. All she said was, "I see. I see."

Then Aunt Rose looked around at the small group sitting at the table as if she had just woken up. She smiled at Lucy and said, "That was a fine breakfast, Lucy. One of your best."

Lucy beamed with pride. Then the two servants realized they had just had their first meal with Miss Rose, and they both reacted in an embarrassed way—Lucy scooping up the dishes and scurrying to the sink, William quickly excusing himself to warm up the car.

"I guess you better be getting to school," Aunt Rose said as she stood up to leave. "I enjoyed our breakfast together."

She picked up the ball and glove.

"I'll just keep these," she added with a smile and left the room.

Jodie gathered her coat, mittens, hat, and scarf off the hook by the backdoor. Lucy smiled her wide, white-toothed grin and wished Jodie a good day. William opened the backdoor for her with the same big grin.

"I knew you were gonna be good for this house," he said. "Yes-s-s sir, I just knew it."

And everyone began the day happy and feeling good. But not everyone ended the day on the same note.

By lunchtime Jodie was feeling really sick. All under her jaw, from her ears to her Adam's apple, was swelling and hurting. Mrs. Rutherford took her temperature, and, yes, Jodie was running a fever. William came right away to take her home, and Lucy quickly met them at the door, whisked Jodie upstairs, and tucked her into bed. Dr. Porter was called in. His check-up was short and painless, announcing after a quick look: mumps. "A lot of it going around. Five cases in the past two weeks." Lucy nodded as the doctor rattled off a list of instructions. All Jodie knew was that she had to stay in bed which was just fine with her. She felt too miserable to do anything else.

Jodie's lower jaws and throat swelled up so much she looked like a chipmunk with a mouth full of nuts. It was hard to talk or eat. She stayed in bed the rest of the day and all the next. By the third day she was feeling just good enough to be bored. That's when she thought of the diary.

She slipped out of bed and pulled out the diary from the bottom drawer where she had meant to keep it hidden away for good. Jodie flipped the pages until she found the entry dated Thanksgiving Day, 1939, crawled back under the covers, and began to read.

Dear Diary,

Today was terrible. Didn't think I would live through it. J.M. came for Thanksgiving dinner. He tried to turn down the invitation, but Rose insisted. She wouldn't let him alone till he said yes. It was just awful. He sat beside Rose. I sat across the table. Every time I looked up J.M. was looking at me with those brown eyes. I nearly choked on my food. Afterwards Rose wanted to play cards, a new game she had learned at college. It was more than I could stand trying to keep my mind on the game with J.M. sitting so close. Our hands touched once on the table, and I was sure Rose could tell what was going on. I pray every night that this will go away or that Rose will find a new boyfriend.

December 11, 1939

Dear Diary,

Only four days until Rose comes home for Christmas. Got a letter from her. She still hopes J.M. will give her an engagement ring. Nothing has gotten better. Only worse. Last Friday J.M. said he loved me. What am I going to do? I know I love him, too. I could never tell Rose. I won't hurt her. I will just have to stop seeing him. There's no other way.

December 27, 1939

Dear Diary,

Have not seen J.M. for a week. There was no engagement ring for Rose. He broke it off two days before Christmas day. It was just awful. She is broken-hearted. All she does is sit in her room and mope. I didn't know what to do. I miss J.M. but can't see him ever again. Rose would just die if I did. I hope she will get over him soon.

January 6, 1940

Dear Diary,

It snowed today. Not much, but enough to cover the ground. I love watching it come down. Rose went back to school yesterday. She is still sad but has not given up hope about J.M. She thinks maybe there's still a chance. She says she may have pushed too hard about the engagement. She plans to write to him. Last night he came to my window and threw rocks at it. I was so afraid he would wake Daddy. I begged him to go home. It was too cold to stand outside. He wanted to meet me on Saturday. I told him no and closed the window. I wish I could say yes. But that's impossible.

January 12, 1940

Dear Diary,

*Had a surprise in church this morning. J.M.
was there. Tried not to look at him but couldn't
help it. Thought he'd be mad because I didn't
meet him on Saturday. After church he slipped
me a note. It says to meet him at the lake at
3:00. It's 2:00 now. What do I do? I'll go
and break it off for good. Then he'll go back to
Rose, and everything will be the way it should
be. That's the only thing I can do.*

Jodie wanted to keep reading, but her eyes were starting to burn, and her neck was aching. She lay back on the pillows and looked at the window. That was the very window her mother had opened on that cold January night. Jodie tried to imagine the sound of the pebbles hitting it, and her daddy standing on the lawn wanting to see the girl inside. She thought how awful her mother must have felt when she closed the window on him. Jodie was no longer angry with her parents. She didn't understand all this love stuff, but it must have been very hard for them to stay apart when they really wanted to be together.

Jodie waited until after Lucy removed her dinner tray from the bed before pulling the diary out from under the covers. She was anxious to finish it. But just as she started to find the place where she had left off, there was a quiet tap on her bedroom door. Jodie quickly shoved the book back under the covers.

Aunt Rose peeked in. "Just wanted to see how you were doing."

With her cheeks still puffy, Jodie managed to reply. "Fine. I'm doing fine." She tried to smile, but her cheeks were so fat her mouth had no room to move. Aunt Rose almost giggled at the funny face, but she stopped herself, smiled, and said good night.

Jodie waited a few minutes to make sure her aunt was gone before uncovering the diary. It was silly, but Jodie didn't want Aunt Rose to see her reading it. Even though her aunt had given the diary to Jodie, it felt like she was peeking through a keyhole to their private lives, and it felt sneaky and wrong.

January 15, 1940

Dear Diary,

Everything is so mixed up. Didn't break it off with J.M. I tried. I really did. I don't know what happened. When I got to the lake he was standing beside the truck. I went up to him to tell him what I thought we should do, and before I knew it he was kissing me. His hands were cold on my face, but I didn't care. I had missed him so much. He kept telling me how much he loved me. I can't tell a living soul about this, and it feels terrible.

March 2, 1940

Dear Diary,

It's been a long time since I've written. Trying to see J.M. as much as possible, but it's very hard. Daddy is starting to ask a lot of questions when I go out. He wonders why I don't go on dates to ballgames and movies. Sue Ellen and Jenny know something is going on. We have to be so sneaky, and I'm tired of it. Got a letter from Rose. Good news. She's going to Atlanta with friends at spring break. I'd go crazy if she were home right now. Her feelings for J.M. haven't changed, and she thinks they will get back together this summer. I miss her, but I would miss J.M. more.

April 6, 1940

Dear Diary,

School in unbearable. It's only a few weeks before graduation, but don't think I can make it. I wish I could just quit and run away with J.M. He asked me to marry him. I don't know what to do. This is not the way things are supposed to be. When you're in love with someone you're supposed to be happy. I cry every day. We want to get married as soon as school is out. I can't do this to Rose. She will hate me. I just know it.

May 7, 1940

Dear Diary,

Today is my birthday. Daddy gave me a beautiful diamond necklace. We had a nice dinner. We all missed Rose, but she will be home from college soon for the whole summer. All Daddy talks about these days is college. He expects me to go to State College just like Rose. I don't think I can go away for a whole year. I would miss J.M. too much. I've been reading some of the things I wrote on the day I got this diary one year ago. I remember all the fun things Rose and I did back then. I wish I could go back to that time. But things have gone too far. It can never be like it was.

May 19, 1940

Dear Diary,

Something terrible happened. Rose came home from school two days early. She left the train station and went straight to see J.M. I'm not exactly sure what he said, but he told her he didn't love her. He told her he had loved someone else since last summer. She came in the house in a terrible fit. Screaming and crying and scaring everyone half to death. She ran into my room and fell across the bed. I could hardly understand a thing she was saying. She is so heart-broken. I can't stand to see her so hurt. Daddy would like to kill J.M. I wish everything would just go away. Maybe I need to go away. I can't stand it any longer.

May 25, 1940

Dear Diary,

*Tomorrow is graduation day. I'm so happy.
It doesn't seem real that I'm finally out of
school. It has been so busy this week. Daddy
is planning to take us on a trip to the coast in
a couple of weeks. I hope it is fun. I haven't
seen J.M. in three days. It's getting harder and
harder to meet. I feel like I'm being watched
all the time. I'm so tired of this secret, tired of
pretending. I don't know the answer.*

May 27, 1940

Dear Diary,

*I don't have much time to write. I'm leaving
tonight with J.M. Everything has gone wrong.
It's terrible. Rose caught J.M. and me together.
She knows that the girl he has loved was me
all along. She hates me. She said so. She never
wants to see me again. She'll never talk to me
for the rest of my life. Daddy was furious.
He ordered me never to see J.M. again. He's
sending me away in a few days. Daddy said
if I don't stop seeing this boy I can never live
under his roof again. I don't care. I love John
Mills, and I'm going to marry him. I would
die if I couldn't see him again. We're going
tonight.*

Jodie flipped through the last few pages of the diary. There
was nothing more written, only blank pages. She was exhausted.
The house was extremely quiet, and she knew without looking at
a clock that it was very late. Though she lay back to fall asleep,
she kept thinking about the story in the diary, her mother's story.
Now she was angry with Aunt Rose. Why did she have to be so
mean to Mama? Why couldn't she just forget about John Mills
and let them be happy? It was too bad that they fell in love with
the same boy, but it wasn't anybody's fault. All the old feelings

about Rose Parker came back. Mama had been forced out of this big house, out of her family, because her sister had been selfish and mean. Mama had given up everything—college, money, home—for the love of John Mills.

It wasn't fair. Jodie wanted to run down the hall and scream at her aunt for causing Mama so much unhappiness. She wanted to run away from this house like her mother had done years ago. How could she ever smile at Aunt Rose again or talk with her at dinner?

She couldn't, and she would have to think of a way out.

chapter fifteen

The winter was a long, cold, gray one. For weeks the sun didn't come out but was hidden behind thick gray clouds. There wasn't any snow, not even a flurry. Each day was as dreary as could be. The temperature was bitter cold. But not as cold as the feelings inside the Parker house.

Jodie built an invisible wall between herself and Aunt Rose, and it puzzled everybody. She stayed in her room most of the time, and when she did sit down for meals, she hardly said two words. Ever since the morning that Aunt Rose came down to the kitchen and ate breakfast with Jodie, Lucy, and William, she began to come down every morning. She enjoyed the company and the conversation. It was like being with family. But that was before Jodie shut out her aunt. Soon Lucy was taking the breakfast tray into the study again. A blanket of gloom fell over the big, white house.

Then one day in the first week of March, the sun decided to pop out bright and warm. The temperature rose, bringing up everybody's spirits with it. Everybody, that is, except Jodie. Today was her birthday, but instead of being excited and happy, she felt pouty and sour. She didn't care if anybody remembered her birthday. She didn't want presents or a cake or any of that stuff. She didn't want to be happy.

At breakfast Lucy and William cut their eyes at each other as Jodie sat down, but they didn't say a word about her birthday, just the usual chit-chat about the weather and school and "My, don't you look nice today, Miss Jodie." She nodded her head and mumbled "thank you" just to be polite and not hurt their feelings, but she was in no mood to talk.

When she got to school she was surprised to find a whole stack of birthday cards piled high on her desk. Her mouth dropped open, and her eyes got big. Despite her determination to be unhappy today, she couldn't keep from smiling. All the fourth graders crowded around her desk. In their eagerness to show Jodie the cards they'd made, they grabbed and poked the cards in Jodie's face for her to read. She was swamped. Mrs. Rutherford had to rescue Jodie by breaking up the mob and getting all the students in their desks. Jodie would have to read the cards later.

All day, everyone was especially nice to Jodie. But, unlike that awful day in the fall when she returned to school, she welcomed the attention. After all, it was her birthday, and even if the people she lived with didn't care, she was glad her schoolmates did. When William picked her up after school, her face was shining as bright as the newly-found sun.

William had a little twinkle in his eye when he said, "Looks like you had a mighty nice day at school."

"Yes, sir, I did," Jodie replied.

And that was all either one of them said on the whole way home. William drove especially slow getting to their house, but Jodie didn't care. She'd rather be in the car thinking about her day than in the house with her aunt. She planned to go straight to her room, dump all the birthday cards on her bed, and get down to reading them.

When she opened the backdoor, the house seemed unusually quiet. Lucy was not at the sink or work table preparing dinner as she normally was. Jodie was disappointed. She had wanted to show Lucy all her birthday cards. She hung up her coat and realized William had not come inside with her. She wanted to show him, too. Something seemed very strange.

There was no after-school snack waiting for her, so she headed down the hall toward the stairs. She was anxious to read her cards. She stopped at the bottom step and listened.

Everything was so quiet. She could hear a strong March breeze blow and shake the windows. The old house creaked as old houses do. But that was all. It gave Jodie the creeps, and her body shivered.

Without warning, Miss Sips came leaping out of the dining room and ran past Jodie up the stairs. It scared her half to death! She jumped and screamed, and before she could even catch her breath, a loud "Surprise!" jolted her again. She threw her books and birthday cards on the stairs and stood there staring at all the faces in the dining room.

What is going on? She saw Lucy and William grinning for all they were worth, showing off their pearly-white teeth. Aunt Rose was holding a birthday cake with ten candles all aglow. And there was Frannie, clapping her hands with excitement, and Ralph standing next to her. *How did they get here?* Jodie could not believe this was happening!

But before she could say anything, everyone began to sing "Happy Birthday" to her. Jodie's face turned red as they sang her name. She'd never had so much attention in her life. Most of her birthdays had been spent quietly, just Mama and herself, and she didn't know what to do or say. When the song was finished, everybody clapped. Frannie grabbed Jodie's arm and dragged her to the table. Jodie stared at the presents sitting there.

"Well, open one," Frannie urged impatiently.

Jodie looked at Aunt Rose to see if it was okay. She nodded her approval as she put the cake on the table. Frannie, who was more eager to see the presents than Jodie was, snatched one up and pushed it in her hands.

Jodie sank down in a chair and laid the present in her lap.

"That one there's from me," William said softly. He smiled. It was hard to hide his pride.

Jodie carefully unwrapped the package and lifted the box lid. Something was packed in newspaper. Taking the small bundle out of the box, she untwisted the newspaper from around it and pulled out a small flute, which had been whittled out of a piece of dark wood and sanded down as smooth as glass. It was beautiful. Jodie held it as if it were pure gold.

"Made it myself," William beamed.

137

"Oh, it's beautiful," Jodie exclaimed. "It's really beautiful."

"Don't be afraid to blow it," William chuckled. "It's made for blowin' and lots of it. Makes a right pretty sound, if I do say so."

Everyone laughed. Jodie put the flute to her lips and gave a big blow. Nothing came out but a big gust of air. She made a face. Everyone laughed again. William took the flute from her hands. He put it to his lips, and out came the prettiest melody you ever heard. He handed it back to her and said, "I'll show you later how it works. We'll practice."

Frannie laid a second present in Jodie's lap before she could even put the flute back in its box. Jodie smiled at her excited friend. Frannie was enjoying this birthday more than Jodie was.

"This one *I* made," Lucy spoke up as Jodie took the paper off. Inside the box were three embroidered handkerchiefs. Lucy's needlework was so neat and pretty and delicate. Jodie remembered how hard it had been to embroider the handkerchief for Aunt Rose. She looked at Lucy with appreciation.

"I love them," she said. And before she could say anything else, another present plopped in her lap. Jodie laughed at her little friend who was so eager to see her presents.

There was a card on this one. Jodie opened the card first and read the message. It read, *I hope you have a wonderful birthday. Love, Aunt Rose.*

Jodie did not want to look at her aunt; she did not want to open the gift from her aunt. But everyone was staring, so she quickly unwrapped it. She gazed at the gift until Frannie could stand it no longer.

"What is it?" she asked. And she pulled Jodie's hand off the box so she could see.

"Oh, my," Frannie exclaimed. She looked at Ralph. "It's a diary."

Ralph was no more excited about a diary than he had been about the flute or handkerchiefs. He just wanted some cake and ice cream.

139

Jodie didn't know what to say. She simply stared at the book in her lap. Aunt Rose came over and stood by Jodie. She laid her hand on Jodie's arm.

"I thought you might like to start a diary," she said sweetly.

For a few seconds Jodie didn't say anything. She just kept staring at the new diary. Then, because Jodie rarely forgot her manners, she thanked Aunt Rose for the gift. There was an awkward silence. Everyone was waiting for something to happen, but nothing did—until Aunt Rose got the party going again by asking Lucy to cut the cake. Ralph's eyes lit up. He had waited long enough.

Later that night, after the half-eaten cake was put away and Jodie's little friends, who were stuffed with it, were driven home, Jodie lay across her bed thinking about the day. She thought about the party and the gifts. It was so different from her birthdays in the past. She thought about life with Mama. They had been poor. Mama worked so hard, but they never had nice things like Jodie had now. She began to get angry again just thinking about Mama. She did not want the nice things; she did not want to live with Aunt Rose. She would not be happy in this house. Not now, not ever. All she wanted to do was get away from this house. Get away from the woman who once caused her mother so much pain.

Jodie jumped up from the bed. She took some clothes out of her drawers and closet and laid them on the quilt on her bed. Then she folded the quilt over the clothes and rolled it up. She opened her bedroom door and listened, but didn't hear a sound. She tiptoed down the stairs, through the hallway, and to the side door. Then she undid the lock above the doorknob and slowly pulled open the door. The cold night air rushed in, and she quickly stepped out onto the porch and closed the door behind her.

Jodie stood for a few minutes on the porch, remembering the day she first brought a rose and laid it here. She wished so badly she could go back to that day that she almost broke down in tears. But she had to go, and go now.

As she slipped across the lawn toward the tall bushes, she wondered if this was what her mother did the night she ran away. Did she run across the dewy grass and through the bushes to a waiting truck? Did her mother feel as scared as Jodie did now? Surely Mama was scared and sad about leaving her home and her family, forever.

Jodie squeezed through the bushes and out onto the sidewalk, not thinking about what to do or where to go. She would go to the only place she knew. She would go home.

chapter sixteen

The rising sun shone brightly through the window. The warm rays fell across Jodie's face and woke her up. She squinted as she tried to open her eyes against the glare of the sun. The room was cold, and the floor was hard. She wrapped her quilt more tightly around her and looked around.

This was her room; she knew it had to be. But it didn't look like the room she had loved so much. The walls were bare, and there was not a piece of furniture anywhere. When she crawled through Mama's bedroom window last night by the light of the moon, she was more frightened than she could have imagined. Her steps echoed in the empty rooms as she searched for something familiar. Her old house was just an empty shell now. There was no warmth, no happiness, no life.

She lay there on the floor, curled up in her quilt, thinking about what had happened. Her stomach growled from hunger, and she wished Lucy were here to fix breakfast. She missed Lucy and William, but she knew she could never go back to Miss Rose's house even if she wanted to.

Just then, Jodie heard a noise. It was a car on the road, and she listened as it drove past. But it didn't drive past. It got closer and closer until Jodie realized it drove right up to her house. She peeked out the window and saw the big black car. *Oh dear!* William was here. How did he know where she was? She would just beg him to go back and say he hadn't found her there.

Jodie watched as the car door on the driver's side slowly opened. She saw feet land on the ground, but they weren't William's. *Oh dear, oh no, oh Lord, please help me!* It was Aunt Rose. And she was coming toward the house.

Jodie's heart beat faster. She looked for a place to hide, but there was nothing here but her clothes and quilt. She couldn't run. Aunt Rose would chase her down in the car. She was trapped and didn't know what to do. This was the end! Aunt Rose would surely send Jodie away now. Or lock her up somewhere. Or worse. She was a goner.

A key turned in the kitchen door, and soon it opened. Jodie heard footsteps coming down the hall. And then there stood Aunt Rose, in the doorway of Jodie's room.

"Jodie, you're here!" Aunt Rose almost screamed. "Thank the Lord, you're safe!" She let out a big gush of air as if trying to catch her breath.

Then something happened. Some horrible thing took over her aunt's body. Her relief turned into rage. And in two giant steps she was on top of Jodie, grabbing her arms with both hands, jerking her up out of the quilt and lifting her body off the floor like a rag doll. Aunt Rose's fingernails dug into Jodie's skin, and she winced in a pain.

"What are you doing?" she screamed. "Don't you know how worried everybody has been? Lucy nearly went into a fit when she found you weren't there. William has been scouring the whole town looking for you. We've all been worried sick."

Aunt Rose had an iron grip on Jodie and was shaking all over with anger; she was shaking the little girl as well. Jodie had never been treated like this before, and she began to cry.

"Haven't we been good to you?" her aunt's rampage continued. "Haven't we given you everything you've needed? I took you into my home, and this is how you repay me?"

Then, just as suddenly as it began, her fit of anger stopped. Aunt Rose looked at Jodie as if seeing her for the first time. In a matter of seconds her face went from angry red to pale as a ghost. She looked horrified and fell on her knees, pulling Jodie to her chest. Wrapping one arm around Jodie's body, Aunt Rose

used the other hand to hold Jodie's head on her shoulder. Then Aunt Rose began to cry uncontrollably.

"Oh, Jodie, I'm so sorry," she sobbed. "I'm so sorry. Please forgive me. I don't know what came over me. I was so afraid I'd lost you. I just. . .I just couldn't bear to lose you."

Jodie was crying, too. She didn't know what to think or what to do. She let Aunt Rose squeeze her, and for a long time, the two cried together. They cried for Mama and the loneliness they both felt. All the sorrow, all the hurt came pouring out in their tears. Jodie found herself hugging Aunt Rose back, and, for a time, it was just the two of them. Everything else had disappeared.

Finally Aunt Rose let Jodie go and dug into her coat pocket to pull out the handkerchief Jodie had made. Aunt Rose wiped the tears from Jodie's face and smoothed back her hair with her fingers. She took off her coat and wrapped it around Jodie who was trembling more from the long cry than from the cold. Once Aunt Rose wiped her own face she said, "Jodie, do you know what the old saying 'bury the hatchet' means?"

Jodie shook her head. She thought it was a silly thing to say at a time like this.

"Well, it means that you forgive someone for a wrong she's done against you," she explained. "You let it go."

Aunt Rose sighed and wiped her eyes. She was starting to cry again. She stood up and turned her back to Jodie but continued to talk.

"I buried all the people who meant everything to me before I buried the hatchet," she sobbed. "It was a terrible mistake. And I've paid a miserable price for it. I'm a fool. A stubborn, prideful fool. I've wasted all of our lives because I was too stubborn to forgive."

She turned to face Jodie.

"You must understand, Jodie," she pleaded. "I loved your mother. She was more dear to me than anybody on earth."

Aunt Rose walked toward Jodie and took her gently by the hand; they both sat down on the quilt in the corner. She put her arms around Jodie, and, without thinking, Jodie laid her head in

145

her aunt's lap just as she had done so many times with Mama. Aunt Rose began to stroke her hair, and Jodie felt comforted. They both sniffed in the silence, trying to get over their hard cry.

Finally Aunt Rose spoke up.

"The night Daisy left with John seemed like the most horrible night of my life. I felt like I'd lost the only two people I would ever love. And they both had hurt me. I was so hurt I didn't know what to do. I felt so betrayed. . .and lost. . .and lonely."

Aunt Rose sat for a few minutes, thinking of the past. Jodie waited quietly.

"Daddy was furious. He felt like he'd lost his daughter, too, I guess. He was a tough old man, but he'd just lost our mother only four years earlier, and I suppose he was reliving all the grief again. Daisy came home three days later. She wanted to say she was sorry. But it was too late. She was married to John, and neither Daddy nor I could forgive her. There was a terrible scene. I could hardly bear to look at her. It was so painful. So I did the unthinkable. I told her to stay away from me forever. I told her I never wanted to see her again, not as long as we lived. And I ran to my room, slammed the door, and locked her out of my life forever."

Aunt Rose used the handkerchief again to wipe her eyes. Jodie could tell she was reliving her memories, and it was still very painful.

"Daddy was even worse. He told Daisy that she was never to come into our house again as long as she was still married to that boy. I don't believe he meant it. I'm sure of that. He was only trying to scare her into leaving John and coming home. He wanted to bully her into being his little girl again. He would have welcomed them both in time, but there was no time. Three months later Daddy died of a heart attack."

Jodie caught her breath. She hadn't expected this part of the story. How awful it must have been for Mama! How awful for Aunt Rose!

"I saw Daisy at the funeral, but we didn't speak. Even in that time of sorrow for both of us, I stood by my word that I would never forgive her. We could have been a great comfort to each other, but my pride wouldn't let me. No, sir, Rose Parker was not giving in. Not on your life."

Aunt Rose shook her head and gave a little snort of disgust at herself.

"I heard some time later that Daisy was going to have a baby. She and John had a nice house on Richmond Street. It was all so perfect for them. I was incredibly jealous, and I let that jealousy and hurt take over my whole being. I swore never to let anyone hurt me like that again. I locked up my heart and threw away the key."

Aunt Rose sat quietly for a while. Jodie was thinking about all Aunt Rose had said. It was hard for Jodie to understand why her aunt couldn't have just made up with Mama and been happy. It made no sense.

Aunt Rose soon continued her story.

"Time passed, and the hardness in me only got worse. Oh, Jodie, I was such a stubborn fool. You were born, and I didn't even go to see you. And when John went away to war, leaving Daisy alone, I was still too mule-headed to make up with her. I felt like she had it all, and it wasn't fair. The older I got, the more stubborn I became. Until I was downright mean and selfish. I got to where I didn't even know how to act any differently. I did everything I could to hurt Daisy because she had hurt me. I'll never forgive myself for not going to your daddy's funeral. When I think of how she had to live. . ."

Aunt Rose broke into tears again. Jodie couldn't help but feel sorry for her aunt. She was in so much pain. Aunt Rose sobbed as if her heart would break. Then she got quiet again. The empty house was as cold and silent as a tomb as Jodie waited for her aunt to continue.

"The mistake with people is. . .you think you've got time. Time to fix things. You think one day *I'll feel better, and I'll walk right up to Daisy's door, and we'll have a good ol' talk and everything will be like it should be.* We could've made up if I'd only reached out. . .like she reached out to me. That's what the Sunday rose was all about, you know. Daisy was asking for forgiveness with each rose. And I kept her locked out."

Jodie sat up and looked at her aunt. Her blue eyes were red from all the crying, and they reflected the terrible hurt and guilt she was feeling. Jodie wanted to do something to help make it go away. She took her aunt's hand and held it. Aunt Rose smiled. But the tears came again.

"Jodie, your mother never needed forgiveness. She hadn't done anything wrong, not really. I was the one who should have begged for her forgiveness. . .and I did. That night when I came over to your house, I made things right. But it was too late. If I had only known. . .if I had known there was little time, I would've done it years before. Oh, Jodie, how could I have been such a fool?" She shook her head and wept. "We always think there's time. How can I ever forgive myself for all those years?"

Jodie could stand it no longer. She had to make her aunt feel better. Somehow she had to make the pain go away. Jodie reached up and gave Aunt Rose a kiss on her cheek. It was the first kiss anybody had given her in a very, very long time, and the distraught woman was stunned. She hugged Jodie very gently; Aunt Rose was finished crying.

"This is the strangest thing of all," Aunt Rose said, wiping her eyes and face. "I thought God was punishing me for being so hard-hearted and selfish by taking away everyone I loved. But then, you came along. God has given you to me. You are a part of Daisy and John and your grandparents. In a way, I'm getting back everyone I love in you. I think it's God's way of telling me that I'm forgiven."

Jodie finally spoke up.

"Then, if God can forgive you, you should do it, too."

Aunt Rose thought about this for a moment. Then she smiled and said, "I guess you're right. Let's go home."

chapter seventeen

It was a beautiful summer day. The sky was clear, and a gentle breeze was stirring just enough to keep the heat down. The big black car rolled to a stop, and the dust blew up in thick clouds around it. The back door opened, and out jumped Jodie. She took off running but stopped suddenly when she heard her aunt call from inside the car.

"You'll need these."

Jodie turned and ran back to the car. Aunt Rose was holding the ball and glove.

"You're right," panted Jodie. "Thanks." Then because she had forgotten earlier, she gave her aunt a big hug and was off again. William backed out the car to find a parking place.

There weren't many people in the bleachers yet and none on the baseball field. Jodie had arrived early, and she was glad; she would have more time to practice. She saw two boys in green and white uniforms pitching a ball back and forth. Looking down at her own green and white uniform, she beamed with pride. Jodie finally made the little league team. She was a Greenwood Gator. Sometimes it comes in handy to be pushy and stubborn and rich. Aunt Rose had used all her powers of persuasion to change some minds about girls and baseball. After all, Aunt Rose had said, it *was* 1951. It was high time women were recognized in this town.

Jodie was trotting past the bleachers when she heard a voice.

"Hey, Jodie. Wait a minute."

She stopped and turned, but no one was there. Then she looked under the bleachers. In the shadows she could see a figure but couldn't make out who it was.

When the figure emerged into the sunlight she saw that it was Tommy the Terrible. He was dressed in a green and white uniform just like hers. Jodie tensed. She knew how he felt about girls and baseball, but she was determined not to let him spoil this day for her.

Tommy stood in front of her. He didn't look angry or mean or threatening. He simply said, "Hi." Jodie returned the greeting, and they stood there awkwardly for a few seconds.

"Uh. . .I just wanted to say," he began nervously. "I wanted to say. . .it's okay you're on the team. I mean. . .well, you're good and all. We could use a good hitter."

Jodie just answered, "Yeah."

"Well, who knows," he shrugged. "We might even win one this year."

They both laughed. Jodie didn't trust Tommy, and she was watching his every move. He might pounce on her any minute. In fact, she could have handled a punch in the face better than what he did give her.

Tommy reached in his back pocket for something. Jodie braced herself. He held out a single red rosebud. Her mouth dropped open in surprise. Her face heated up, and she blushed.

"Here," he said. "It's. . .it's for you. . .a good luck charm. You know, like a four-leaf clover. You keep it. . .you know, for good luck."

Tommy was blushing, too. He started to back away, and, as he turned to go, he added, "See ya' after the game. Maybe we can go to Pete's for a Coke." And he was gone.

Jodie hadn't said anything because she was so shocked she couldn't breathe. She stared at the rose in her hand. Because she

had always thought boys were stupid and stingy and mean, what just happened knocked her for a loop.

Jodie walked slowly toward the baseball field, studying the tiny rose. It made her think of Mama. She still missed her mother something awful, and she knew she always would. But the memories had begun to make her feel happy rather than sad, and she knew that the memories would always be with her.

The rose also confused Jodie. She didn't understand all this stuff about falling in love. It only seemed to make a mess of everything. It made people do things they didn't want to do. It had surely tangled up a mess for Mama and Aunt Rose.

But Jodie knew one day she just might fall in love. She didn't want to lock up her heart and throw away the key like Aunt Rose had done. Even if it meant she might get hurt. Jodie knew that one day she would probably write *mushy* stuff in her own diary. Maybe even about Tommy who wasn't a bit terrible anymore. But it would be a long time from now.

Right now, she had her little friend, Frannie, her new family, and baseball. That was enough. Putting the rose in her shirt pocket, Jodie knew she would keep it, even though she had had plenty of roses in her life.

Soon the bleachers filled with people. Jodie shaded her eyes and tried to find Aunt Rose in the crowd. It wasn't hard. There she sat with a big floppy hat on her head. Beside her were William, who was still looking very starched in his white shirt even without his suit coat, and Lucy who had worn a pretty lilac dress and white shoes. Jodie waved at them before she stepped up to the plate. She dug her heels into the dirt and took her stance. The pitcher was winding up.

"This one's for you, Mama," she whispered to herself. And she knocked that ball clean out of the park.

THE END

about the author

For thirty years Nancy has been teaching children to read. During this time she has read thousands of children's stories with her students and her granddaughters. Combining this love for reading and her love for writing she decided to write her own stories that she hoped children would enjoy.

Nancy lives in Memphis, Tennessee, with her husband, Earl. Their two daughters and two granddaughters also live in the city. She has a Bachelor's degree from Arkansas State University and a Master's degree in education from the University of Memphis. She currently teaches at Presbyterian Day School.

During the years of Nancy's childhood there were few opportunities for young girls to play organized sports. One goal of *The Secret and the Sunday Rose* is to give young girls today a glimpse into this restricted world through her character, Jodie. Nancy also shares in this book the intrigue of family secrets, a diary that unlocks the past, and a deep tragedy. The story reveals life in a time that, though not so long ago, is so very different from today.

Rebel In Petticoats

In 1861 ten-year-old Rachel Franklin and her family are pulled into the midst of the Civil War. Though at first the glory of fighting for the southern Cause brought pride and excitement into the Franklin home, the truth of war's hardships soon become apparent. Before the war the biggest worries for Rachel were using proper manners and controlling her jealousy towards her brother Bud's sweetheart, Suzanna Wade. Now Rachel and her mother must work the gardens, pick cotton, tend to their wounded men, and wait between letters with only hope that their loved ones survive. "We must be strong," Mama tells her, and on the night when Rachel must deliver an important message for Papa to save the lives of countless men, she learns the true meaning of bravery when she becomes a little *Rebel in Petticoats*.

http://rebelinpetticoats.com/

To purchase books by this author, visit www.omorepublishing.com.

The World of Ivy

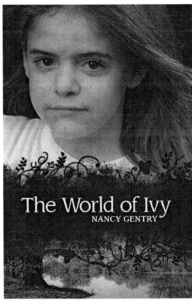

It is May of 1940 as Ivy finishes her 5th grade year in the Tucker's Bayou of Arkansas. Ivy loves learning but hates school. She doesn't fit in with those silly, prissy girls in their fancy lace dresses; she'd much rather wear her cutoff jeans and a white tee-shirt. Her teacher favors Linda Sue — the most girly and prissy of them all. School is also a place where she has to endure Danny, a bully whose brothers are even more terrifying than he is.

Ivy would much rather stay at home with Granpa J and Little Mary, her faithful beagle, enjoying a visit from Miss Dotty, who often brings over homemade muffins and other great foods. She prefers summertime, when she can fish at her secret spot by the creek.

But an afternoon at her secret spot brings about changes Ivy never expected; she discovers a new friend, Esau, who isn't allowed to go to school because he isn't white. Ivy takes it on as a personal mission to teach Esau to read, and she's surprised to find help from a new teacher in town. Still, is this town ready for such a change? She's always been different, but what will this challenge of a lifetime do to *The World of Ivy*?

To purchase books by this author visit www.omorepublishing.com.

CPSIA information can be obtained at www.ICGtesting.com
Printed in the USA
243734LV00005B/1/P